UNANIMOUS ACCLAIM FOR THE FIRST
IN A NEW GENERATION OF HORROR
NOVELS—

"A STRIPPED-DOWN, TERRIFYING STO-
ry. You will shudder...but read on without
stopping!"

—*Saturday Review*

"A BRILLIANT AND SINISTER *TOUR DE
force* about adolescent sexuality and expression..."

—A. Alvarez

"A RIVETING NOVEL FROM ITS OPEN-
ing paragraph. I could not put it down. It
possesses the suspense and chilling impact of
*Lord of the Flies!*"

—*Washington Post*

"McEWAN HAS ALREADY CREATED A
style and a vision of life of his own. *The Cement
Garden* is further proof of his remarkable
powers!"

—John Fowles

# THE CEMENT GARDEN

# IAN McEWAN
# THE CEMENT GARDEN

A BERKLEY BOOK
published by
BERKLEY PUBLISHING CORPORATION

This Berkley book contains the complete
text of the original hardcover edition.
It has been completely reset in a type face
designed for easy reading, and was printed
from new film.

THE CEMENT GARDEN

A Berkley Book / published by arrangement with
Simon and Schuster

PRINTING HISTORY
Simon and Schuster edition published 1978
Berkley edition / January 1980

ISBN: 0-425-04496-3

A BERKLEY BOOK® TM 757,375
Berkley Books are published by Berkley Publishing Corporation,
200 Madison Avenue, New York, New York 10016.
PRINTED IN THE UNITED STATES OF AMERICA

**For Penny**

# IAN McEWAN THE CEMENT GARDEN

# Part One

# Chapter One

I DID NOT kill my father, but I sometimes felt I had helped him on his way. And but for the fact that it coincided with a landmark in my own physical growth, his death seemed insignificant compared to what followed. My sisters and I talked about him the week after he died, and Sue certainly cried when the ambulance men tucked him up in a bright red blanket and carried him away. He was a frail, irascible, obsessive man with yellowish hands and face. I am only including the little story of his death to explain how my sisters and I came to have such a large quantity of cement at our disposal.

In the early summer of my fourteenth year a lorry pulled up outside our house. I was sitting on the front step rereading a comic. The driver and another man came toward me. They were covered in a fine, pale dust which gave their faces a ghostly look. They were both whistling shrilly completely different tunes. I stood up and held the comic out of sight. I wished I had been reading the racing page of my father's paper or the football results.

"Cement?" one of them said.

I hooked my thumbs into my pockets, moved my weight onto one foot and narrowed my eyes a little. I wanted to say something terse and appropriate, but I was not sure I had heard them right. I left it too long, for the one who had spoken rolled his eyes toward the sky and with his hands on his hips stared past me at the front door. It opened and my father stepped out, biting on his pipe and holding a clipboard against his hip.

"Cement," the man said again, this time with a downward inflection. My father nodded. I folded the comic into my back pocket and followed the three men up the path to the lorry. My father stood on tiptoe to look over the side, took his pipe from his mouth and nodded again. The man who had not yet spoken made a savage chop with his hand. A steel pin flew free and one side of the lorry fell away with a great noise. The tightly packed paper sacks of cement were arranged two deep along the floor of the lorry.

My father counted them, looked at his clipboard and said, "Fifteen." The two men grunted. I liked this kind of talk. I too said to myself, "Fifteen." The men took a sack each on their shoulders and we went back down the path, this time with me in front followed by my father. Round to one side of the house he pointed with the wet stem of his pipe at the coal hole. The men heaved their sacks into the cellar and returned to their lorry for more. My father made a mark on the clipboard with a pencil which dangled from it by a piece of string. He rocked back on his heels, waiting. I leaned against the fence. I did not know what the cement was for, and I did not wish to be placed outside this intense community of work by showing ignorance. I counted the sacks too, and when they were all done I stood at my father's elbow while he signed the delivery note. Then without a word he returned indoors.

That night my parents argued over the bags of cement. My mother, who was a quiet sort of person, was furious. She wanted my father to send the whole lot back. We had just finished supper. While my mother talked my father used a penknife to scrape black shards from the bowl of his pipe onto the food he had barely touched. He knew how to use his pipe against her. She was telling him how little money we had and that Tom would soon be needing new clothes for starting at school. He replaced the pipe between his teeth like a missing section of his own anatomy and interrupted to say it was "out of the question" sending the bags back and "that is the end of it." Having seen for myself the lorry and the heavy sacks and the men who had brought them, I sensed he was right. But how self-important and foolish he looked as he took the thing out of his mouth, held it by its bowl and pointed the black stem at my mother. She became angrier, her voice choked with exasperation. Julie, Sue and I slipped away upstairs to Julie's bedroom and closed the door. The rise and fall of our mother's voice reached

5

us through the floor, but the words themselves were lost.

Sue lay on the bed giggling with her knuckles in her mouth while Julie pushed a chair against the door. Together we rapidly stripped Sue of her clothes and when we were pulling down her pants our hands touched. Sue was rather thin. Her skin clung tightly to her rib cage and the hard muscular ridge of her buttocks strangely resembled her shoulder blades. Faint gingerish down grew between her legs. The game was that Julie and I were scientists examining a specimen from outer space. We spoke in clipped Germanic voices as we faced each other across the naked body. From downstairs came the tired, insistent drone of our mother's voice. Julie had a high ridge of cheekbone beneath her eyes which gave her the deep look of some rare wild animal. In the electric light her eyes were black and big. The soft line of her mouth was just broken by two front teeth, and she had to pout a little to conceal her smile. I longed to examine my older sister but the game did not allow for that.

"Vell?" We rolled Sue onto her side and then onto her belly. We stroked her back and thighs with our fingernails. We looked into her mouth and between her legs with a torch and found the little flower made of flesh.

"Vot do you think of zis, Herr Doctor?" Julie stroked it with a moistened finger and a small tremor ran along Sue's bony spine. I watched closely. I moistened my finger and slid it over Julie's.

"Nothing serious," she said at last, and closed the slit with her finger and thumb. "But ve vill votch for further developments, *ja?*" Sue begged us to go on. Julie and I looked at each other knowingly, knowing nothing.

"It's Julie's turn," I said.

"No," she said as always. "It's your turn."

Still on her back, Sue pleaded with us. I crossed the room, picked up Sue's skirt and threw it at her.

"Out of the question," I said through an imaginary pipe. "That's the end of it."

I locked myself in the bathroom and sat on the edge of the bath with my pants round my ankles. I thought of Julie's pale brown fingers between Sue's legs as I brought myself to my quick, dry stab of pleasure. I remained doubled up after the spasm passed and became aware that downstairs the voices had long ago ceased.

THE NEXT morning I went down into the cellar with Tom, my younger brother. It was large and divided into a number of meaningless rooms. Tom clung to my side as we descended the stone stairs. He had heard about the cement bags and now he wanted to look at them. The coal hole gave onto the largest of the rooms and the bags were strewn as they had fallen over what remained of last year's coal. Along one wall was a massive tin chest, something to do with my father's brief time in the Army, and used for a while to hold the coke separate from the coal. Tom wanted to look inside, so I lifted the lid for him. It was empty and blackened, so black that in this dusty light we could not see the bottom. Believing he was staring into a deep hole, Tom gripped the edge and shouted into the trunk and waited for his echo.

When nothing happened he demanded to be shown the other rooms. I took him to one nearer the stairs. The door was almost off its hinges and when I pushed it, it came away completely. Tom laughed and had his echo at last returned to him from the room we had just left. In this room there were cardboard boxes of mildewed clothes, none of them familiar to me. Tom found some of his old toys. He turned them over contemptuously with his foot and told me they were for babies. Heaped up behind the door was an old brass cot that all of us had slept in at one time or another. Tom wanted me to reassemble it for him and I told him that cots were for babies too.

At the foot of the stairs we met our father coming down. He wanted me, he said, to give him a hand with the sacks. We followed him back into the large room. Tom was scared of Father and kept well behind me. Julie had told me recently that now Father was a semi-invalid he would have to compete with Tom for Mother's attention. It was an extraordinary idea and I thought about it for a long time. So simple, so bizarre, a small boy and a grown man competing. Later I asked Julie who would win and without hesitation she said, "Tom of course, and Dad'll take it out on him."

And he was strict with Tom, always going on at him in a needling sort of way. He used Mother against Tom much as he used his pipe against her. "Don't talk to your mother like that" or "Sit up straight when your mother is talking to you." She took all this in silence. If Father then left the room, she would smile briefly at Tom or tidy his hair with her fingers. Now Tom stood back from the doorway watching us drag each sack between us across the floor, arranging them in two neat lines along the wall. Because of his heart attack my father was forbidden this sort of work, but I made sure he took as much weight as I did.

When we bent down and each took hold of a corner of a sack, I felt him delay, waiting for me to take up the strain. But I said, "One two three..." and pulled only when I saw his arm stiffen. If I were to do more then I wanted him to acknowledge it out loud. When we were done, we stood back like workers do, looking at the job. My father leaned with one hand against the wall breathing heavily. I deliberately breathed as lightly as I could, through my nose, even though it made me feel faint. I kept my hands casually on my hips.

"What do you want all this for?" I felt I now had a right to ask.

He snatched at words between breaths. "For ...the garden." I waited for more but after a pause he turned to leave. In the doorway he caught hold of Tom's arm.

"Look at the state of your hands," he complained, unaware of the mess his own hand was making on Tom's shirt. "Go on, up you go."

I remained behind a moment and then began turning off the lights. Hearing the clicks, so it seemed to me, my father stopped at the foot of the stairs and reminded me sternly to turn off all the lights before I came up.

"I already was," I said irritably. But he was coughing loudly on his way up the stairs.

He had constructed rather than cultivated his garden according to plans he sometimes spread out

9

on the kitchen table in the evenings while we peered over his shoulder. There were narrow flagstone paths which made elaborate curves to visit flower beds that were only a few feet away. One path spiraled up round a rockery as though it were a mountain pass. It annoyed him once to see Tom walking straight up the side of the rockery, using the path like a short flight of stairs.

"Walk up it properly," he shouted out the kitchen window. There was a lawn the size of a card table raised a couple of feet on a pile of rocks. Round the edge of the lawn there was just space for a single row of marigolds. He alone called it the hanging garden. In the very center of the hanging garden was a plaster statue of a dancing Pan. Here and there were sudden flights of steps, down, then up. There was a pond with a blue plastic bottom. Once he brought home two goldfish in a plastic bag. The birds ate them the same day. The paths were so narrow it was possible to lose your balance and fall into the flower beds. He chose flowers for their neatness and symmetry. He liked tulips best of all and planted them well apart. He did not like bushes or ivy or roses. He would have nothing that tangled. On either side of us the houses had been cleared and in summer the vacant sites grew lush with weeds and their flowers. Before his first heart attack he had intended to build a high wall round his special world.

There were a few running jokes in the family, initiated and maintained by my father. Against Sue for having almost invisible eyebrows and lashes, against Julie for her ambitions to be a famous athlete, against Tom for pissing in his bed sometimes, against Mother for being poor at arithmetic and against me for my pimples which were just starting up at that time. One suppertime I passed him a plate of food and he remarked that he did not want his food to get too close to my face. The laughter was instant and ritual. Because little jokes like this one were stage-managed by Father, none of them ever worked against him.

That night Julie and I locked ourselves in her bedroom and set to work filling pages with crude overworked jokes. Everything we thought of seemed funny. We fell from the bed to the floor, clutching at our chests, screeching with delight. Outside Tom and Sue were banging on the door demanding to be let in. Our best jokes were, we thought, the question and answer ones. Several of them made references to Father's constipation. But we knew the real target. We selected our best, polished it and practiced it. Then we waited a day or two. It was supper, and as it happened he came out with another crack about my spots. We waited for Tom and Sue to stop laughing. My heart was beating so hard it was difficult to sound casual, conversational, the way we had rehearsed it. I said, "I saw something out in the garden today that gave me a shock."

"Oh," said Julie, "what was that?"

"A flower."

No one seemed to hear us. Tom was talking to himself, Mother poured a little milk into her cup and Father continued to butter with extreme care the slice of bread before him. Where butter strayed over the edge of his bread he folded it back with a quick sliding movement of his knife. I thought perhaps we should say it again louder and I looked across at Julie. She would not meet my eye. Father finished his bread and left the room.

Mother said, "That was quite unnecessary."

"What was?"

But she said nothing more to me. Jokes were not made against Father because they were not funny. He sulked. I felt guilt when I desperately wanted to feel elation. I tried to convince Julie of our victory so that she in turn would convince me. We had Sue up that night lying between us, but the game was giving us no pleasure. Sue got bored and went away. Julie was for apologizing, making it up to him in some way. I could not face that, but when, two days later, he spoke to me for the first time, I was greatly relieved. Then the garden was not mentioned for a long time, and when he covered the kitchen table with his plans he looked at them alone. After his first heart attack he stopped work on the garden altogether. Weeds pushed up through the cracks in the paving stones. Part of the rockery collapsed and the little pond dried up. The dancing Pan fell on its side and broke in two, and nothing was said. The possibility that Julie and I were responsible for the disintegration filled me with horror and delight.

Shortly after the cement came the sand. A pale yellow pile filled one corner of the front garden. It became apparent, probably through my mother, that the plan was to surround the house, front and back, with an even plane of concrete. My father confirmed this one evening.

"It will be tidier," he said. "I won't be able to keep up the garden now"—he tapped his left breast with his pipe—"and it will keep the muck off your mother's clean floors." He was so convinced of the sanity of his ideas that through embarrassment rather than fear, no one spoke against the plan. In fact, a great expanse of concrete round the house appealed to me. It would be a place to play football. I saw helicopters landing there. Above all, mixing concrete and spreading it over a leveled garden was a fascinating violation. My excitement increased when my father talked of hiring a cement mixer.

My mother must have talked him out of that for we started work one Saturday morning in June with two shovels. In the cellar we split open one of the paper sacks and filled a zinc bucket with the fine pale gray powder. Then my father went outside to take the bucket from me as I passed it up through the coal hole. When he reached forward, he made a silhouette against the white featureless sky behind him. He emptied the powder on the path and returned it to me for refilling. When we had enough of that, I wheeled a barrow load of sand from the front and added it to the pile. His plan was to make a hard path round the side of the house so that it would be easy to move sand from the front garden to the back. Apart from his infrequent, terse instructions, we said nothing. I was pleased that we knew so exactly what we were doing and what the other was thinking that we did not need to speak. For once I felt at ease with him. While I fetched water in the bucket he shaped the cement and sand into a mound with a dip in its center. I did the mixing while he added the water. He showed me how to use the inside of my knee against my forearm to gain better leverage. I pretended that I knew already. When the mix was consistent we spread it on the ground. Then my father went down on his knees and smoothed the surface with the flat side of a short plank. I stood behind him, leaning on my shovel. He stood up and supported himself against the fence and closed his eyes. When he opened them he blinked as if he was surprised to find himself here and said, "Well, let's get on then." We repeated the operation, the bucket loads through the coal hole, the wheelbarrow, the water, the mixing and spreading and smoothing.

The fourth time round boredom and familiar longings were slowing my movements. I yawned frequently, and my legs felt weak behind the knees. In the cellar I put my hands in my pants. I wondered where my sisters were. Why weren't they helping? I passed a bucketful to my father and then, addressing myself to his shape, told him I needed to go to the toilet. He sighed and at the same time made a noise with his tongue against the roof of his mouth. Upstairs, aware of his impatience, I worked on myself rapidly. As usual, the image before me was Julie's hand between Sue's legs. From downstairs I could hear the scrape of the shovel. My father was mixing the cement himself. Then it happened, it appeared quite suddenly on the back of my wrist, and though I knew about it from jokes and school biology books, and had been waiting for many months, hoping that I was no different from any other, now I was astonished and moved. Against downy hairs, lying across the edge of a gray concrete stain, glistened a little patch of liquid, not milky as I had thought, but colorless. I dabbed at it with my tongue and it tasted of nothing. I stared at it a long time, up close to look for little things with long, flickering tails. As I watched it dried to a barely visible shiny crust which cracked when I flexed my wrist. I decided not to wash it away.

I remembered my father waiting and I hurried downstairs. My mother, Julie and Sue were standing about talking in the kitchen as I passed through. They did not seem to notice me. My father was lying face down on the ground, his head resting on the newly spread concrete. The smoothing plank was in his hand. I approached slowly, knowing I had to run for help. For several seconds I could not move away. I stared wonderingly, just as I had a few minutes before. A light breeze stirred a loose corner of his shirt.

Subsequently there was a great deal of activity and noise. An ambulance came, and my mother went off in it with my father who was laid out on a stretcher and covered with a red blanket. In the living room Sue cried and Julie comforted her. The radio was playing in the kitchen. I went back outside after the ambulance had left to look at our path. I did not have a thought in my head as I picked up the plank and carefully smoothed away his impression in the soft, fresh concrete.

# Chapter Two

DURING THE following year Julie trained for the school athletics team. She already held the local under-eighteen records for the 100- and 220-yard sprint. She could run faster than anyone I knew. Father never took her seriously, he said it was daft in a girl, running fast, and not long before he died he refused to come to a sports meeting with us. We attacked him bitterly; even Mother joined in. He laughed at our exasperation. Perhaps he really intended to be there, but we left him alone and sulked among ourselves. On the day, because we did not ask him to come, he forgot and never saw, in the last month of his life, his oldest daughter star of all the field. He missed the pale brown slim legs flickering across the green like blades, or me, Tom, Mother and Sue running across the enclosure to cover Julie with kisses when she took her third race. In the evenings she often stayed at home to wash her hair and iron pleats in her navy blue school skirt. She was one of a handful of daring girls at school who wore starched white petticoats beneath their skirts to fill them out and make them swirl when they turned on their heel. She wore stockings and black knickers, strictly forbidden. She had a clean white blouse five days a week. Some mornings she gathered her hair in the nape of her neck with a brilliant white ribbon. All this took considerable preparation each evening. I used to sit around, watching her at the ironing board, getting on her nerves.

She had boyfriends at school, but she never really let them get near her. There was an unspoken family rule that none of us ever brought friends home. Her closest friends were girls, the most rebellious, the ones with reputations. I sometimes saw her at school at the far end of a corridor surrounded by a small noisy group. But Julie herself gave little away; she dominated her group and heightened her reputation with a disruptive, intimidating quietness. I had some status at school as Julie's brother but she never spoke to me there or acknowledged my presence.

At some point during the same period my spots were so thoroughly established across my face that I abandoned all the rituals of personal hygiene. I no longer washed my face or hair or cut my nails or took baths. I gave up brushing my teeth. In her quiet way my mother reproved me continuously, but I now felt proudly beyond her control. If people really liked me, I argued, they would take me as I was. In the early morning my mother came into my bedroom and exchanged my dirty clothes for clean ones. On weekends I lay in bed till the afternoon and then took long solitary walks. In the evenings I watched Julie, listened to the radio or just sat. I had no close friends at school.

I frequently stared at myself in mirrors, some-times for as long as an hour. One morning, shortly before my fifteenth birthday, I was searching in the gloom of our huge hallway for my shoes when I glimpsed myself in a full-length mirror which leaned against the wall. My father had always intended to secure it. Colored light through the stained glass above the front door illuminated from behind stray fibers of my hair. The yellowish semidarkness obscured the humps and pits of my complexion. I felt noble and unique. I stared at my own image till it began to dissociate itself and paralyze me with its look. It receded and returned to me with each beat of my pulse, and a dark halo throbbed above its head and shoulders. "Tough," it said to me. "Tough." And then louder, "shit ... piss ... arse." From the kitchen my mother called my name in weary admonition.

From a bowl of fruit I picked out an apple and went to the kitchen. I slouched in the doorway and watched the family at breakfast and tossed the apple in my hand, catching it with crisp smacks against the palm. Julie and Sue read schoolbooks while they were eating. My mother, drained by another night without sleep, was not eating. Her sunken eyes were gray and watery. With whines of irritation Tom was trying to push his chair nearer hers. He wanted to sit in her lap, but she complained he was too heavy. She arranged the chair for him and ran her fingers through her hair.

The issue was whether Julie would walk to school with me. We used to go together every morning, but now she preferred not to be seen with me. I continued to toss the apple, imagining it made them all uneasy. My mother watched me steadily.

"Come on Julie," I said at last. Julie refilled her teacup.

"I've got things to do," she said firmly. "You go on."

"What about you then, Sue?"

My younger sister did not look up from her book. She murmured, "Not going yet."

My mother reminded me gently that I had not had my breakfast but I was already on my way through the hall. I slammed the front door hard and crossed the road. Our house had once stood in a street full of houses. Now it stood on empty land where stinging nettles grew round torn corrugated tin. The other houses were knocked down for a motorway they never built. Sometimes kids from the tower blocks came to play near our house, but usually they went farther up the road to the empty prefabs to kick the walls down and pick up what they could find. Once they set fire to one, and no one cared very much. Our house was old and large. It was built to look a little like a castle, with thick walls, squat windows and crenellations above the front door. Seen from across the road it looked like the face of someone concentrating, trying to remember.

No one ever came to visit us. Neither my mother nor my father when he was alive had any real friends outside the family. They were both only children, and all my grandparents were dead. My mother had distant relatives in Ireland whom she had not seen since she was a child. Tom had a couple of friends he sometimes played with in the street, but we never let him bring them in the house. There was not even a milkman in our road now. As far as I could remember, the last people to visit the house had been the ambulance men who took my father away.

I stood there several minutes wondering whether to return indoors and say something conciliatory to my mother. I was about to move on when the front door opened and Julie slipped out. She wore her black gabardine school raincoat belted tightly about her waist and the collar was turned up. She turned quickly to catch the front door before it slammed and the coat, skirt and petticoat spun with her, the desired effect. She had not seen me yet. I watched her sling her satchel over her shoulder. Julie could run like the wind, but she walked as though asleep, dead slow, straight-backed and in a very straight line. She often appeared deep in thought, but when we asked her she always protested that her mind was empty.

She did not see me until she was across the road and then she half smiled, half pouted and remained silent. Her silence made us all a little afraid of her, but again she would protest, her voice musical with bemusement, that *she* was the one who was afraid. It was true, she was shy—there was a rumor she never spoke in class without blushing—but she had the quiet strength and detachment and lived in the separate world of those who are, and secretly know they are, exceptionally beautiful. I walked alongside her and she stared ahead, her back straight as a ruler, her lips softly pursed.

A hundred yards on, our road ran into another street. A few terraced houses remained. The rest, and all the houses in the next street across, had been cleared to make way for four twenty-story tower blocks. They stood on wide aprons of cracked asphalt where weeds were pushing through. They looked even older and sadder than our house. All down their concrete sides were colossal stains, almost black, caused by the rain. They never dried out. When Julie and I reached the end of our road I lunged at her wrist and said, "Carry your satchel, miss." Julie pulled her arm away and went on walking. I danced backward in her path. Her brooding silences turned me into a nuisance.

"Wanna fight? Wanna race?" Julie lowered her eyes and kept to her course. I said in a normal voice, "What's wrong?"

"Nothing."

"Are you pissed off?"

"Yes."

"With me?"

"Yes."

I paused before speaking again. Already Julie was drifting away, absorbed in some internal vision of her anger. I said, "Because of Mum?" We were drawing level with the first of the tower blocks and we could see through into the lobby. A gang of kids from another school were gathered around the lift shaft. They lolled against the walls without talking. They were waiting for someone to come down in the lift. I said, "I'll go back then." I stopped. Julie shrugged and made a sudden movement with her hand that made it clear she was leaving me behind.

Back on our street I met Sue. She walked with a book held open in front of her. Her satchel was strapped tight and high across her shoulders. Tom walked a few yards behind. From the look on his face it was clear there had been another scene getting him out of the house. I felt easier with Sue. She was two years younger than I, and if she had secrets I was not intimidated by them. Once I saw in her bedroom a lotion she had bought to "dissolve" her freckles. Her face was long and delicate, the lips colorless and the eyes small and tired-looking with pale, almost invisible lashes. With her high forehead and wispy hair she sometimes really did look like a girl from another planet. We did not stop, but as we passed Sue looked up from her book and said, "You're going to be late."

And I muttered, "Forgot something." Tom was preoccupied with his own dread of school and did not notice me. The realization that Sue was taking him to school to save Mother the walk increased my guilt, and I walked faster.

I walked round the side of the house to the back garden and watched my mother through one of the kitchen windows. She sat at the table with the mess of our breakfast and four empty chairs in front of her. Immediately facing her was my untouched bowl of porridge. One hand was in her lap, the other on the table, the arm crooked as if ready to receive her head. Near her was a squat black bottle which contained her pills. Her face mixed Julie's features with Sue's, as though she were their child. The skin was smooth and taut over the fine cheekbones. Each morning she painted on her lips a perfect bow in deepest red. But her eyes, set in dark skin wrinkled like a peach stone, were sunk so far into her skull she seemed to stare out from a deep well. She stroked the thick dark curls at the back of her head. On some mornings I would find a nest of her hair floating in the toilet. I always flushed it away first. Now she stood up and with her back to me began to clear the table.

When I was eight years old I came home from school one morning pretending to be seriously ill. My mother indulged me. She put me into my pajamas, carried me to the sofa in the living room and wrapped me in a blanket. She knew I had come home to monopolize her while my father and two sisters were out of the house. Perhaps she was glad to have someone at home with her during the day. Till the late afternoon I lay there and watched as she went about her work, and when she was in another part of the house I listened closely. I was struck by the obvious fact of her independent existence. She went on, even when I was away at school. These were the things she did. Everybody went on. At that time the insight had been memorable but not painful. Now, as I watched her stoop to knock eggshells from the table into the rubbish pail, the same, simple recognition conveyed both sadness and menace, in unbearable combination. She was not a particular invention of mine, or of my sisters, though I continued to invent and ignore her. As she was moving an empty milk bottle, she turned suddenly toward the window. I stepped back quickly. As I ran down the side path I heard her open the back door and call my name. I caught a glimpse of her as she stepped round the corner of the house. She called after me again as I set off down the street. I ran all the way, imagining her voice above the row of my feet on the pavement.

"Jack . . . Jack."

I caught up with my sister Sue just as she was turning through the school gates.

# Chapter Three

I KNEW IT was morning, and I knew it was a bad dream. By an effort of will I could wake myself. I tried to move my legs, to make one foot touch the other. Any slight sensation would be enough to establish me in the world outside my dream. I was being followed by someone I could not see. In their hands they carried a box, and they wanted me to look inside, but I hurried on. I paused for a moment and attempted to move my legs again or open my eyes. But someone was coming with the box, there was no time and I had to run on. Then we came face to face. The box, wooden and hinged, might once have contained expensive cigars. The lid was lifted half an inch or so, too dark to see inside. I ran on in order to gain time, and this time I succeeded in opening my eyes. Before they closed, I saw my bedroom, my school shirt lying across a chair, a shoe upside down on the floor. Here was the box again. I knew there was a small creature inside, kept captive against its will and stinking horribly. I tried to call out, hoping to wake myself with the sound of my own voice. No sound left my throat, and I could not even move my lips. The lid of the box was being lifted again. I could not turn and run for I had been running all night and now I had no choice but to look inside. With great relief I heard the door of my bedroom open and footsteps across the floor. Someone was sitting on the edge of my bed, right by my side, and I could open my eyes.

My mother sat in such a way as to trap my arms inside the bedclothes. It was half past eight by my alarm and I was going to be late for school. My mother would have been up for two hours already. She smelled of the bright pink soap she used. She said, "It's time we had a talk, you and I." She crossed one leg over the other and rested her hands on her knees. Her back, like Julie's, was very straight. However ill she was, she always sat very straight. I felt at a disadvantage lying on my back, and I struggled to sit up. But she said, "You lie there a moment."

"I'm going to be late," I said.

"You lie there a moment," she repeated with a heavy emphasis on the last word. "I want to talk to you."

My heart beating very fast, I stared past her head at the ceiling. I was barely out of my dream.

"Look at me," she said. "I want to look at your eyes."

I looked into her eyes and they roved anxiously across my face. I saw my own swollen reflection.

"Have you looked at your eyes in a mirror lately?" she said.

"No," I said untruthfully.

"Your pupils are very large, did you know that?" I shook my head. "And there are bags under your eyes even though you've just woken up." She paused. Downstairs I could hear the others eating breakfast. "And do you know why that is?" Again I shook my head, and again she paused. She leaned forward and spoke urgently. "You know what I'm talking about don't you?" My heart thudded in my ears.

"No," I said.

"Yes you do, my boy. You know what I'm talking about, I can see you do."

I had no choice but to confirm this with my silence. This sternness did not suit her at all; there was a flat, playacting tone in her voice, the only way she could deliver her difficult message.

"Don't think I don't know what's going on. You're growing into a young man now, and I'm very proud you are . . . these are things your father would have been telling you. . . ." We looked away; we both knew this was not true. "Growing up is difficult, but if you carry on the way you are, you're going to do yourself a lot of damage, damage to your growing body."

"Damage . . ." I echoed.

"Yes, look at yourself," she said in a softer voice.

"You can't get up in the mornings, you're tired all day, you're moody, you don't wash yourself or change your clothes, you're rude to your sisters and to me. And we both know why that is. Every time. . . ." She trailed away and, rather than look at me, stared down at her hands in her lap. "Every time . . . you do that, it takes two pints of blood to replace it." She looked at me defiantly.

"Blood," I whispered. She leaned forward and kissed me lightly on the cheek.

"You don't mind me saying this to you, do you?"

"No, no," I said. She stood up.

"One day, when you're twenty-one, you'll turn round and thank me for telling you what I've been telling you." I nodded. She stooped over me and affectionately ruffled my hair and then quickly left the room.

My sisters and I no longer played together on Julie's bed. The games ceased not long after Father died, although it was not his death that brought them to an end. Sue became reluctant. Perhaps she had learned something at school and was ashamed of herself for letting us do things to her. I was never certain because it was not something we could talk about. And Julie was more remote now. She wore makeup and had all kinds of secrets. In the dinner queue at school I once overheard her refer to me as her "kid brother," and I was stung. She had long conversations with Mother in the kitchen that would break off if Tom, Sue or I came in suddenly. Like my mother, Julie made remarks to me about my hair or my clothes, not gently though, but with scorn.

"You stink," she would say whenever there was

disagreement between us. "You really do stink. Why don't you ever change your clothes?" Remarks like these made me loutish.

"Fuck you," I would snarl, and go for her ankles, determined to tickle her until she died of exhaustion.

"Mum," she would shriek, "Mum, tell Jack!"

And my mother would call tiredly from wherever she happened to be, "Jack...."

The last time I tickled Julie I waited till Mother was at the doctor's; then I slipped on a huge, filthy pair of gardening gloves, last worn by my father, and followed Julie up to her bedroom. She was sitting at the small desk she used for doing homework on. I stood in the doorway with my hands behind my back.

"What do you want?" she said in full disgust. We had been quarreling downstairs.

"Come to get you," I said simply, and spread my enormous hands toward her, fingers outstretched. The sight alone of these advancing on her made her weak. She tried to stand up, but she fell back in her chair.

"You dare," she kept saying through her rising giggles. "You just dare."

The big hands were still inches from her, and she was writhing in her chair, squealing. "No...no ...no."

"Yes," I said, "your time has come." I dragged her by the arm onto her bed. She lay with her knees drawn up, her hands raised to protect her throat. She dared not take her eyes off the great hands which I held above her, ready to swoop down.

"Get away from me," she whispered. It struck me

31

as funny at the time that she addressed the gloves and not me.

"They're coming for you," I said, and lowered my hands a few inches. "But no one knows where they will strike first."

Feebly she tried to catch at my wrists. I slid my hands under hers, and the gloves clamped firmly round her rib cage, right into the armpits. As Julie laughed and laughed, and fought for air, I laughed too, delighted with my power. Now there was an edge of panic in her thrashing about. She could not breathe in. She was trying to say "please," but in my exhilaration I could not stop. Air still left her lungs in little birdlike clucks. One hand plucked at the coarse material of the glove. As I moved forward to be in a better position to hold her down, I felt hot liquid spreading over my knee. Horrified, I leaped from the bed and shook the gloves from my hands. Julie's last laughs tailed away into tired weeping. She lay on her back, tears spilling over the trough of her cheekbones and losing themselves in her hair. The room smelled only faintly of urine. I picked up the gloves from the floor.

Julie turned her head. "Get out," she said dully.

"Sorry," I said.

"Get . . . out."

Tom and Sue were in the doorway, watching.

"What happened?" Sue asked me as I came out.

"Nothing," I said, and closed the door very quietly.

It was about this time that Mother more and more frequently went to bed in the early evening. She said she could barely keep awake.

"A few early nights in a row," she would say, "and I'll be myself again."

This left Julie in charge of supper and bedtime. Sue and I were in the living room listening to the radio. Julie came in and snapped it off.

"Empty the rubbish bucket will you," she said to me, "and carry the dustbins round to the front."

"Piss off," I shouted, "I was listening to that," and reached for the control knob.

Julie covered it with her hand. I still felt too shamed by my assault on her to struggle with her. A few words of token resistance and I was outside carrying the dustbins. When I returned Sue was at the kitchen sink peeling potatoes. Later, when we sat down to eat, there was strained silence instead of the usual row. When I looked across at Sue she giggled. Julie would not look at us, and when she spoke it was in a low voice to Tom. When she left the room for a minute to take a tray of food upstairs, Sue and I kicked each other under the table and laughed. But we stopped when we heard her coming back down.

Tom did not like these evenings without his mother. Julie made him eat everything on his plate, and he was not permitted to crawl under the table or make funny noises. What outraged him most was that Julie would not let him in Mother's bedroom while she was sleeping. He liked to climb in beside her with all his clothes on. Julie caught him by his wrist on his way upstairs.

"Not up there," she said quietly. "Mum's asleep."

Tom set up a terrible howl, but he did not resist when Julie dragged him back into the kitchen. He too was a little afraid of her. She was suddenly so remote from us, quiet, certain of her authority. I wanted to say to her, "Come on Julie, stop pretending. We know who you are really." And I kept looking her way. But there was no answering look. She kept busy and her eyes met mine only briefly.

I avoided being alone with my mother in case she spoke to me again. I knew from school she had got it wrong. But every time I set to now, once or twice a day, there passed through my mind the image of two pint milk bottles filled with blood and capped with silver foil. I was spending more time with Sue. She seemed to like me, or at least was prepared to ignore me. She passed much of her time at home reading in her bedroom, and she never objected to me lying around in there. She read novels about girls her own age, thirteen or so, who had adventures at their boarding schools. From the local library she borrowed large, illustrated books about dinosaurs or volcanoes or the fish of tropical seas. Sometimes I thumbed through them, looking at the pictures. None of the information interested me. I was suspicious of the paintings of dinosaurs, and I told Sue that no one could really know what they looked like. She told me about skeletons and all the clues there were to help in a reconstruction. We argued all afternoon. She knew far more than I, but I was determined not to let her win. Finally, bored and exasperated, we became sulky and left each other alone. But most often we talked like conspirators, about the family and all the other people we knew, careful scrutinies of their behavior and appearance, what they were "really like." We wondered how ill our mother was. Sue had overheard her tell Julie that she was changing her doctor again. We agreed that our older sister was getting above herself. I did not really think of Sue as a girl now. She was, unlike Julie, merely a sister, a person. One long Sunday afternoon Julie came in during a conversation we were having about our parents. I had been saying that secretly they had hated each other and that Mother was relieved when Father died. Julie sat on the bed next to Sue, crossed her legs and yawned. I paused and cleared my throat.

"Go on," Julie said, "it sounds interesting."

I said, "It wasn't anything."

"Oh," said Julie. She flushed a little and looked down. Now Sue cleared her throat, and we all waited.

I said foolishly, "I was just saying I don't think Mum ever really liked Dad."

"Didn't she?" Julie said with mock interest. She was angry.

"I don't know," I muttered. "Perhaps you know."

"Why should I know?"

There was another silence. Then Sue said, "'Cause you talk to her more than we do."

Julie's anger expressed itself in mounting silence. She stood up and when she had crossed the room she turned in the doorway and said quietly, "Only because you two won't have anything to do with her."

She paused by the door waiting for a reply, and then she was gone, leaving behind a very faint smell of perfume.

The next day, after school, I offered to walk down to the shops with my mother.

"There's nothing to carry," she said. She was standing in the gloomy hallway, knotting her scarf in the mirror.

"Feel like a walk," I mumbled.

We walked in silence for several minutes; then she linked her arm through mine and said to me, "It's your birthday soon."

I said, "Yeah, pretty soon."

"Are you excited about being fifteen?"

"Dunno," I said.

While we waited in a chemist's shop for a prescription for my mother I asked her what the doctor had said. She was examining a gift-wrapped bar of soap in a plastic dish. She put it down and smiled cheerily.

"Oh, they're all talking rubbish. I've done with the lot of them." She nodded toward the pharmaceutical counter. "As long as I get my pills."

I felt relieved. The prescription came at last in a heavy brown bottle which I offered to carry for her. On the way home she suggested we have a little party on my birthday and that I invite a few friends from school.

"No," I said immediately. "Let's just have the family."

For the rest of the way home we made plans, and we were both glad to have at last something to talk about. My mother remembered a party we had had on Julie's tenth birthday. I remembered it too; I was eight. Julie had wept because someone had told her that there were no more birthdays after you were ten. It had become for a while a family joke. Neither of us mentioned the effect my father had had on that and all the other parties I could remember. He liked to have the children stand in neat lines waiting their turn at some game he had set up. Noise and chaos, children milling around without purpose, irritated him profoundly. There was never a birthday party during which he did not lose his temper with someone. At Sue's eighth birthday party he tried to send her to bed for fooling around. Mother intervened, and that was the last of the parties. Tom had never had one. By the time we reached our front gate we had fallen silent. As she fumbled in her handbag for a front door key, I wondered if she was glad that this time we would be having a party without him.

I said, "Pity Dad couldn't be...."

And she said, "Poor dear. He would have been so proud of you."

Two days before my birthday my mother took to her bed.

"I'll be up in time," she said when Sue and I went in to see her. "I'm not ill, I'm just very, very tired."

Even as she was speaking to us her eyes were barely open. She had already made a cake and iced it with concentric circles of red and blue. In the very center stood one candle. Tom was amused by this.

"You're not fifteen," he shouted, "you're only one when it's your birthday."

Early in the morning Tom came into my room and jumped on my bed.

"Wake up, wake up, you're one today."

At breakfast Julie handed me, without comment, a small leather pouch which contained a metal comb and nail scissors. Sue gave me a science fiction novel. On its cover a great, tentacled monster was engulfing a spaceship and beyond the sky was black, pierced by bright stars. I took a tray up to my mother's room. When I went in she was lying on her back and her eyes were open. I sat on the edge of her bed and balanced the tray on my knees. She sat propped up by pillows, sipping her tea. Then she said, "Happy birthday, son. I can't speak in the mornings till I've had something to drink."

We embraced clumsily over the teacup she still held in her hand. I opened the envelope she gave me. Inside a birthday card were two pound notes. On the card was a still-life photograph of a globe, a pile of old leather-bound books, fishing tackle and a cricket ball. I embraced her again and she said "oops" as the cup wobbled in its saucer. We sat together for a while and she squeezed my hand. Her own was yellowish and scrawny, like a chicken's foot, I thought.

All morning I lay on my bed reading the book Sue had given me. It was the first novel I had ever read all the way through. Minute life-bearing spores drifting in clouds across galaxies had been touched by special rays from a dying sun and had latched onto a colossal monster who fed off x-rays and who was now terrorizing regular space traffic between Earth and Mars. It was Commander Hunt's task not only to destroy this beast but to dispose of its gigantic corpse.

"To allow it to drift forever through space," explained one scientist to Hunt at one of their many briefings, "would not only create a collision hazard, but who knows what other cosmic rays might do to their rotten bulks? Who knows what other monstrous mutation might emerge from this carcass?"

When Julie came into my room and told me that Mother was not getting up and that we were having the cake round her bedside, I was so engrossed that I stared at her without comprehension.

"Why don't you do her a favor," Julie said as she was leaving, "and clean yourself up for once?"

In the afternoon Tom and Sue carried the cake and cups upstairs. I locked myself in the bathroom and stood in front of the mirror. I was not the kind Commander Hunt would have had on board his spaceship. I was trying to grow a beard to conceal my skin, yet each of the sparse hairs led the eye like a pointing finger to the spot at its base. I filled the washbasin with hot water and leaned with my immersed palms taking my weight against the bottom of the sink. I often passed half an hour this way, inclined toward the mirror, my hands and wrists in hot water. It was the closest I came to washing. I daydreamed instead, this time about Commander Hunt. When the water was no longer hot I dried my hands and took from my pocket the little leather pouch. I cut my fingernails and combed my lank brown hair, experimenting with different styles and deciding at last to celebrate my birthday with a center parting.

As I entered my mother's bedroom, Sue started singing "Happy Birthday," and the others joined in. The cake rested on the bedside table and its candle was already lit. My mother lay surrounded by pillows, and though she was moving her lips to the song, I could not make out her voice. When they were done, I blew out the candle and Tom danced before the bed and chanted, "You're one, you're one," till Julie shushed him.

"You look very smart," my mother said. "Have you just had a bath?"

"Yes," I said, and cut the cake.

Into the teacups Sue poured the orange juice she had made, she said, from four pounds of real oranges.

"All oranges are real, aren't they Mum?" Tom said.

We all laughed and Tom, delighted with himself, repeated his remark several times but with diminishing success. It was hardly a party really, and I was impatient to return to my book. Julie had arranged four chairs in a shallow curve facing one side of the bed, and there we sat, nibbling the cake and sipping the juice. Mother ate and drank nothing. Julie wanted something to happen; she wanted us to be entertaining.

"Tell us a joke," she said to Sue, "the one you told me yesterday."

And when Sue had told her joke and Mother had laughed, Julie said to Tom, "Show us all your cartwheel."

We had to move the chairs and plates out of the way so that Tom could fool around on the floor and giggle. Julie made him stop after a while, and then she turned to me.

"Why don't you sing us a song?"

I said, "I don't know any songs."

"Yes, you do," she said. "What about 'Greensleeves'?"

The very title of the song irritated me. "I wish

you'd stop telling people what to do," I said. "You're not God are you?"

Sue intervened. "*You* do something, Julie," she said.

While Julie and I were talking Tom had taken his shoes off and climbed into bed beside Mother. She had put her arm around his shoulder and was watching us as if we were a long way off.

"Yeah," I said to Julie, "you do something for a change."

Without a word Julie launched herself into the space cleared for Tom's cartwheels, and suddenly her body was upside down, supported only by her hands, taut and lean and perfectly still. Her skirt fell down over her head. Her knickers showed a brilliant white against the pale brown skin of her legs, and I could see how the material bunched in little pleats around the elastic that clung to her flat, muscular belly. A few black hairs curled out from the white crotch. Her legs, which were together at first, now moved slowly apart like giant arms. Julie brought her legs together again and, dropping them to the floor, stood up. In a confused, wild moment I found myself on my feet singing "Greensleeves" in a trembling, passionate tenor. When I finished they all clapped and Julie squeezed my hand. Mother was smiling drowsily. Everything was cleared away quickly; Julie lifted Tom out of the bed, Sue carried away the plates and the remains of the cake and I took the chairs.

# Chapter Four

ONE HOT afternoon I found a sledgehammer lying concealed by weeds and long grass. I was in the garden of one of the abandoned prefabs, poking around, bored. The building itself had been gutted by fire six months before. I stood inside the blackened living room where the ceiling had collapsed and the floorboards burned away. One partitioned wall remained and in its center was a serving hatch connecting with the kitchen. One of its small wooden doors was still on its hinges. In the kitchen, broken sections of water pipe and electrical fittings clung to the wall, and on the floor was a smashed sink. In all the rooms tall weeds were struggling for the light. Most houses were crammed with immovable objects in their proper places, and each object told you what to do—here you ate, here you slept, here you sat. But in this burned-out place there was no order; everything had gone. I tried to imagine carpets, wardrobes, pictures, chairs, a sewing machine, in these gaping smashed-up rooms. I was pleased by how irrelevant, how puny, such objects now appeared. There was a mattress in one room, buckled between the blackened, broken joists. The wall was crumbling away round the window, and the ceiling had fallen in without quite reaching the ground. The people who slept on that mattress, I thought, really believed they were in "the bedroom." They took it for granted that it would always be so. I thought of my own bedroom, of Julie's, my mother's, all rooms that would one day collapse. I had climbed over the mattress and was balancing on a ridge of broken wall, thinking about this, when I saw the handle of the sledgehammer in the grass. I jumped down and seized it. Gray wood lice had been living under the massive iron head and now they ran backward and forward in blind confusion across the little patch of earth. I swung the hammer down on them and felt the ground shake beneath my feet.

It was a good find, probably left by the firemen or a demolition team. I balanced it over my shoulder and carried it home, wondering what I could usefully smash up. In the garden the rockery was disintegrating and overgrown. There was nothing to lay into apart from the paving stones, and they were already cracked. I decided on the cement path— fifteen feet long and a couple of inches thick. It was serving no purpose. I stripped down to the waist and set to. A little concrete crumbled away on the first blow, but the next few produced nothing, not even a crack. I rested and began again. This time, surprisingly, a great fissure opened up and a large, satisfying piece of concrete came away. It was about two feet across and heavy to lift. I pulled it clear and rested it against the fence. I was about to pick up the hammer again when I heard Julie's voice behind me.

"You're not to do that."

She was wearing a bright green bikini. In one hand she held a magazine and in the other her sunglasses. Round this side of the house we were in deep shade. I rested the hammerhead on the ground between my feet and leaned on the handle.

"What are you talking about?" I said. "Why not?"

"Mum said."

I picked up the hammer and swung it at the path as hard as I could. I looked over my shoulder at my sister who shrugged and was walking away.

"Why?" I called after her.

"She's not feeling well," said Julie without turning round. "She's got a headache."

I swore and rested the hammer against the wall.

I had accepted without curiosity the fact that Mother was rarely out of bed now. She became bedridden so gradually we hardly commented on it. Since my birthday, two weeks before, she had not been up at all. We adapted well enough. We took it in turns to take up the tray, and Julie shopped on the way back from school. Sue helped her cook and I washed the dishes. Mother lay surrounded by magazines and library books, but I never saw her reading. Most of the time she dozed in a sitting-up position, and when I came in she would wake up with a little start and say something like: "Oh, I must have dropped off for a moment."

Because there were no visitors, there was no one to ask us what was wrong with her, and so I did not really put the question clearly to myself. Julie, it turned out, knew far more. Every Saturday morning she took the prescription for renewal and came back with the brown bottle full once more. No doctors came to see Mother. "I've seen enough doctors and I've had enough tests to last me a lifetime." It seemed reasonable to me to tire of doctors.

Her bedroom became the center of the house. We would be there, talking among ourselves or listening to her radio, while she dozed. Sometimes I heard her giving Julie instructions about the shopping or Tom's clothes always in a soft and rapid undertone. "When Mother gets up" became a vague, unsought-for time in the near future when the old patterns would be reestablished. Julie appeared serious and efficient, but I suspected she was exploiting the position, that she enjoyed ordering me about. "It's about time you cleaned up your room," she said to me one weekend.

"What do you mean?"

"It's a mess, it smells in there of something." I said nothing. Julie went on, "You better clean it up. Mum said."

Because my mother was ill I thought that I should do what she asked, and while I did nothing to my room I thought about it, I worried about cleaning it up. Mother never mentioned my room to me, and I began to think she had never said anything to Julie.

After staring at my sledgehammer for a minute or two, I walked round to the back garden. It was mid-July, only a week before the summer holidays began, and it had been hot every day for six weeks. It was difficult to imagine it ever raining again. Julie was anxious to be suntanned and had cleared a little flat patch on top of the crumbling rockery. Each day she spread out her bath towel for an hour after school. She would lie with her hands and fingers flattened on the ground beside her, and every ten minutes or so she turned over onto her belly, hooking loose with her thumbs her bikini straps. She liked to set off her deepening color with a white school blouse. She had just settled down again as I came round the corner. She lay on her belly, head cradled on her forearms and face turned away from me toward the wasteland next door where great clusters of stinging nettles were dying of thirst. At her side, lodged between her sunglasses and a thick tube of suntan lotion, was a miniature transistor radio, silver and black, from which came the thin, rattling sound of male voices. The sides of the rockery dropped sharply away from where she was lying. A slight movement to her left and she would be rolling down toward my feet. The shrubs and weeds were withered, and her bikini, brilliant and luminescent, was all that was green on the rockery.

"Listen," I said to her over the radio voices.

She did not turn her head my way, but I knew she had heard me.

"When did Mum tell you to tell me to stop making that noise?"

Julie did not move or speak so I clambered round the rockery in order to see her face. Her eyes were open.

"I mean, you've been out here all the time."

But Julie said, "Do me a favor, will you, and rub some lotion on my back."

As I climbed up my foot dislodged a large rock and it thudded to the ground.

"Careful," Julie said.

I knelt between her open legs and squirted from the tube a pale creamy fluid onto my palm.

"Up by my shoulders and neck," said Julie, "is where it needs it most," and dropping her head she lifted her hair clear of her nape.

Although we were only five feet above the ground, up here there seemed to be a slight and refreshing breeze. As I rubbed the cream into her shoulders I noticed how pale and grubby my own hands appeared against her back. Her shoulder straps were untied and trailed on the ground. If I moved a little to one side, I could just make out her breasts, obscure in the deep shade of her body. When I had finished she called over her shoulder, "Now do my legs."

This time I rubbed the cream on as quickly as I could, with my eyes half closed. I felt hot and sick in the stomach. Julie's head was resting once more on her forearm and her breathing was slow and regular, like someone asleep. From the radio a piping voice was recounting racing results with malicious monotomy. As soon as her legs were adequately coated I jumped down off the rockery.

"Thanks," Julie called out to me sleepily.

I hurried indoors and upstairs to the bathroom. Later that evening I threw the sledgehammer down into the cellar.

•   •   •

EVERY THREE mornings it was my turn to walk Tom to his school. It was always difficult to get him to go. Sometimes he screamed and kicked and had to be carried out of the house. One morning, shortly before the end of term, he told me quite calmly as we walked along that he had an "enemy" at school. The words sounded eerie on his lips and I asked him what he meant. He explained that there was a bigger boy out to get him.

"He's gonna bash my head in," he said in a tone close to wonderment.

I was not surprised. Tom was just the kind to be picked on. He was small for a six-year-old, and frail. He was pale, a little jug-eared, had an idiotic grin and black hair which grew in a thick, lopsided fringe. Worse, he was clever in a niggling, argumentative way—the perfect playground victim.

"You tell me who he is," I said, straightening my slumping back, "and I'll sort him out."

We stopped outside the school and peered through the black railings.

"That one," he said at last and pointed in the direction of a small wooden shed. It was a scrawny-looking kid, a couple of years older than Tom, red-headed and freckled. The meanest sort, I thought. I crossed the playground at great speed and seized him by his lapel with my right hand and, with the other gripped round his throat, banged him hard against the shed and pinned him there. His face shook and seemed to bulge. I wanted to laugh out loud, so wild was my elation.

"You lay a finger on my brother," I hissed, "and I'll rip your legs off." Then I let him go.

It was Sue who brought Tom home from school that afternoon. His shirt was hanging in shreds off his back, and one of his shoes was gone. One side of his face was swollen and red, and a corner of his mouth was torn. Both his knees were grazed, and dried blood ran in streaks down his shin. His left hand was swollen and tender, as though it had been trodden on. As soon as he got in the house Tom began a strange animal howl and made for the stairs.

"Don't let Mum see him like that," Julie shouted.

We were on him like a pack of hounds onto a wounded rabbit. We carried him into the downstairs bathroom and shut the door. With all four of us in there we did not have much space and in the hollow acoustic of this room Tom's cries were deafening. Julie, Sue and I pressed around him, kissing and caressing him as we undressed him. Sue was almost crying too.

"Oh Tom," she kept saying over and over again, "our poor little Tom." With all this going on, I still managed to feel envy for my naked brother. Julie sat on the edge of the bath and Tom stood between her knees, leaning back against her while she dabbed at his face with cotton wool. Her free hand steadied him, the palm flat against his belly, just above the groin. Sue held a cold flannel against his bruised hand.

"Was it that ginger kid?" I said.

"No," Tom wailed. "His friend."

Once he was cleaned up he did not look so badly hurt, and the sense of drama ebbed away. Julie wrapped him in a bath towel and carried him upstairs. Sue and I went ahead to prepare Mother. She must have heard something because she was out of bed and in her dressing gown, ready to come down.

"Just a little scrap at school," we told her. "But he's all right now."

She got back into bed and Julie put Tom in beside her. Later, as we sat around the bed talking about what had happened and drinking tea, Tom, still wrapped in the bath towel, fell asleep.

We were downstairs one evening after supper. Both Tom and Mother were already asleep. Mother had sent Julie to Tom's school that day to talk to the class teacher about the bullying, and we had been talking about that. Sue told Julie and me that she had had the "weirdest" conversation with Tom. Sue waited for one of us to prompt her.

"What did he say then?" I said wearily after half a minute had gone by. Sue giggled.

"He told me not to tell anyone."

"You'd better not then," Julie said, but Sue went on.

"He came into my room and said, 'What's it like being a girl?' and I said it's nice, why? And he said he was *tired* of being a boy and he wanted to be a girl now. And I said but you can't be a girl if you're a boy, and he said, 'Yes, I can. If I want to, I can.' So then I said why do you want to be a girl? And he said, 'Because you don't get hit when you're a girl.' And I told him you do sometimes, but he said, 'No you don't, no you don't.' So then I said how can you be a girl when everyone knows you're a boy, and he said, 'I'll wear a dress and make my hair like yours and go in the girls' entrance.' So I said he couldn't do that, and he said yes, he could, and then he said he wanted to anyway, he wants...."

Sue and Julie were laughing so much now that it was not possible for Sue to continue her story. I did not even smile. I was horrified and fascinated.

51

"Poor little thing," Julie was saying. "We should let him be a girl if he wants to."

Sue was delighted. She clapped her hands together. "He'd look so beautiful in one of my old frocks. That sweet little face."

They looked at each other and laughed. There was a strange excitement in the air.

"He'd look bloody idiotic," I said suddenly.

"Yes?" Julie said coolly. "Why do you think that?"

"You know he would...." There was a pause; Julie was gathering and shaping her anger. Her bare arms lay across the table, a deeper brown than ever under the electric light.

"Making him look stupid," I muttered when I sensed I should be silent, "just so you can have a laugh."

Julie spoke quietly. "You think girls look idiotic, daft, stupid...?"

"No," I said indignantly.

"You think it's humiliating to look like a girl, because you think it's humiliating to *be* a girl."

"It would be for Tom, to look like a girl."

Julie took a deep breath and her voice dropped to a murmur. "Girls can wear jeans and cut their hair short and wear shirts and boots because it's okay to be a boy; for girls it's like promotion. But for a boy to look like a girl is degrading, according to you, because secretly you believe that being a girl is degrading. Why else would you think it's humiliating for Tom to wear a frock?"

"Because it is," I said determinedly.

"But why?" Julie and Sue called together, and before I could think of anything Julie said, "If I wore your trousers to school tomorrow and you wore my skirt, we'd soon see who had the worse time. Everyone would point at you and laugh." Here Julie pointed across the table, her fingers inches from my nose.

"Look at him! He looks just like...ugh!...a *girl!*"

"And look at her"—Sue was pointing at Julie—"she looks rather...*clever* in those trousers." My two sisters laughed so hard they collapsed in each other's arms.

It was simply a theoretical discussion, for one day later Tom was back at school and his teacher wrote Mother a long letter. She read parts of it out loud while Sue and I were maneuvering the dining-room table into her bedroom.

"Tom is a pleasure to have in the class." Mother read this line over a couple of times with great satisfaction. She also liked "He is a gentle but spirited child." We had decided to eat our meals in the bedroom with Mother. I carried up two small armchairs too and now there was barely space to move around the bed. Reading the letter exhausted her. She lay back against the pillows, holding her glasses loosely in one hand. The letter slid to the floor. Sue picked it up and pushed it back into the envelope.

"When I'm up," Mother said to her, "we'll redecorate the downstairs room before we put all this furniture back." Sue sat on her bed and they talked about color schemes. I sat at the table, leaning on my elbows. It was late afternoon and still very hot. Both the sash windows in the bedroom were open as far as they could go. From outside there were the sounds of kids playing round the empty prefabs farther up the street, sudden shouts above the murmur of voices, someone's name being called. There were a lot of flies in the room. I watched one crawl the length of my arm. Julie was sunning herself on the rockery and Tom was out playing somewhere.

Mother had fallen asleep. Sue took the glasses out of her hand, folded them and placed them on the bedside table, and then she left the room. I listened to the rise and fall of my mother's breathing. A particular arrangement of mucus in her nose caused a faint, high-pitched sound like a sharp blade in the air, and then that faded. To have the dining-room table up here was still a novelty to me. I could not quite leave it. I saw for the first time the swirling black lines of the wood's grain beneath the dark lacquer stain. I rested my bare arms along its cool surface. It seemed more substantial here and I could no longer imagine it downstairs. From her bed my mother made a brief, soft chewing sound with her tongue against her teeth, as though she were dreaming of being thirsty. Finally I went and stood by the window, yawning frequently. I had homework to do, but since the long summer holiday was about to begin I no longer cared. I was not even sure if I wanted to return to school in the autumn, and yet I had no plans to do anything else. Outside, Tom and another boy about his size pulled a large lorry tire along the street till they were out of sight. The fact that they were dragging it along and not rolling it made me feel immensely weary.

I was about to sit down at the table again when my mother called my name, and I went to sit on her bed. She smiled and touched my wrist. I moved my hand between my knees. I did not want to be touched; it was too hot.

"What are you up to?" she asked.

"Nothing," I told her through a sigh.

"Fed up?" I nodded. She tried to stroke me with her hand but I was sitting just out of her reach.

. "Let's hope you can find yourself a job for the holidays, get yourself a little pocket money." I grunted ambiguously and briefly turned my face toward her. Her eyes, as always, were sunk deep, and the skin around her eyes was dark and convoluted, as though it too were a seeing surface. Her hair was thinner and grayer; a few strands of it lay on the sheet. She wore a grayish pink cardigan over her nightdress, and its sleeve bulged at the wrist because she kept her handkerchiefs tucked in there.

"Sit a little nearer, Jack," she said. "There's something I want to tell you and I don't want the others to hear." I moved up the bed and she rested her hand on my forearm.

A minute or two passed and she did not speak. I waited, a little bored, a little suspicious that she wanted to talk to me about my appearance or my squandered blood. If it was to be that, I was ready to walk away from the bed and out of the room. At last she said, "I might have to go away soon."

"Where?" I said instantly.

"To the hospital to give them a chance to get to the bottom of whatever it is I've got."

"How long for?" She paused, and her eyes moved from mine and stared over my shoulder.

"It might be quite a long time. That's why I want to talk to you." I was more interested in how long she really meant; a sense of freedom was tugging at my concern. But she was saying, "It really means that Julie and you will have to be in charge."

"You mean Julie will." I was sullen.

"Both of you," she said firmly. "It's not fair to leave it all to her."

"You tell her then," I said, "that I'm in charge too."

"The house must be run properly, Jack, and Tom has to be looked after. You've got to keep things clean and tidy; otherwise you know what will happen."

"What?"

"They'll come and put Tom into care, and perhaps you and Susan too. Julie wouldn't stay here by herself. So the house would stand empty, the word would get around and it wouldn't be long before people would be breaking in, taking things, smashing everything up." She squeezed my arm and smiled. "And then when I come out of the hospital there would be nothing for us all to come back to." I nodded. "I've opened an account at the post office for Julie, and money will get paid into it from my savings. There's enough for you all for quite a while, easily enough till I come out of hospital." She settled back against the pillows and half closed her eyes. I stood up.

"Okay," I said. "When do you go in?"

"It might not be for a week or two yet," she said without opening her eyes. As I reached the door she said, "The sooner the better, I think."

"Yes."

The different position of my voice made her open her eyes. I stood at the door, ready to leave. She said, "I'm tired of lying here doing nothing all day."

Three days later she was dead. Julie found her
when she got in from school on Friday afternoon,
the last day of the summer term. Sue had taken Tom
swimming, and I arrived back minutes after Julie.
As I turned down our front path I saw her leaning
out of Mother's window and she saw me, but we
ignored each other. I did not go upstairs immediately. I took my jacket and shoes off and drank a glass
of cold water from the tap in the kitchen. I looked in
the refrigerator for something to eat, found some
cheese and ate it with an apple. The house was very
quiet and I felt oppressed by the empty weeks ahead.
I had not found a job yet; I had not even looked for
one. Out of habit, I went upstairs to say hello to my
mother. I found Julie on the landing just outside
Mother's bedroom, and when she saw me she pulled
the door shut and stooped to lock it. Trembling
slightly, she stood facing me, the key clenched
tightly in her fist.

"She's dead," Julie said evenly.

"What do you mean? How do you know?"

"She's been dying for months." Julie pushed past
me on the stairs. "She didn't want you lot to know."
I resented "you lot" immediately.

"I want to see," I said. "Give me that key." Julie
shook her head.

"You better come down and talk before Tom and
Sue get in."

For a moment I thought of snatching at the key,
but I turned and, light-headed, close to blasphe-
mous laughter, followed my sister down.

# Chapter Five

BY THE time I got to the kitchen Julie had already arranged herself there. She had tied her hair in a ponytail and was leaning back against the sink, her arms folded. All her weight was on one foot, and the other rested flat against the cupboard behind her so that her knee protruded.

"Where have you been?" she said, but I did not understand her.

"I want to see," I said. Julie shook her head. "We're both in charge," I said as I circled the kitchen table, "she told me."

"She's dead," Julie said, "Sit down. Don't you understand yet? She's dead." I sat down.

"I'm in charge too," I said, and began to cry

because I felt cheated. My mother had gone without explaining to Julie what she had told me. Not to hospital, but gone completely, and there could be no verification. For a moment I perceived clearly the fact of her death, and my crying became dry and hard. But then I pictured myself as someone whose mother had just died and my crying was wet and easy again. Julie's hand was on my shoulder. As soon as I became aware of it I saw, as though through the kitchen window, the unmoving tableau we formed, sitter and stander, and I was unsure briefly which was me. Someone below me sat weeping at the end of my fingers. I was uncertain whether Julie was waiting tenderly or impatiently for me to stop crying. I did not know if she was thinking of me at all for the hand on my shoulder was neutral in touch. This uncertainty made me stop crying. I wished to see the expression on her face. Julie resumed her position by the sink and said, "Tom and Sue will be here." I wiped my face and blew my nose on the kitchen towel. "We might as well tell them as soon as they get in." I nodded, and we stood about, waiting in silence, for almost half an hour.

When Sue came in and Julie told her the news, both girls burst into tears and embraced each other. Tom was still outside somewhere. I watched my sisters crying; I sensed it would seem hostile to look elsewhere. I felt excluded but I did not wish to appear so. At one point I placed my hand on Sue's shoulder, the way Julie had on mine, but neither of them noticed me, any more than wrestlers in a clinch would, so I removed it. Through their crying Julie and Sue were saying unintelligible things, to themselves perhaps or to each other. I wished I could abandon myself like them, but I felt watched. I wanted to go and look at myself in the mirror. When Tom came in the girls separated and turned their faces. He demanded a glass of squash, drank it and left. Sue and I followed Julie upstairs, and while we were standing behind her on the landing, waiting for her to open the door, I thought of Sue and myself as a married couple about to be shown into a sinister hotel room. I belched, Sue giggled and Julie made a shushing noise.

The curtains were not drawn in order, Julie told me later, to "avoid suspicion." The room was full of sunlight. Mother lay propped up by pillows, her hands under the sheet. She could have been about to doze off, for her eyes were not open and staring like dead people's in films, nor were they competely closed. On the floor near the bed were her magazines and books, and on the bedside table there was an alarm clock which still ticked, a glass of water and an orange. While Sue and I watched from the foot of the bed, Julie took hold of the sheet and tried to draw it over Mother's head. Because she was sitting up, the sheet would not reach. Julie pulled harder, the sheet came loose and she was able to cover the head. Mother's feet appeared; they stuck out from underneath the blanket, bluish white with a space between each toe. Sue and I giggled again. Julie pulled the blanket over the feet and Mother's head was revealed once more like an unveiled statue. Sue and I laughed uncontrollably. Julie was laughing too; through clenched teeth her whole body shook. The bedclothes were finally in place, and Julie came and stood by us at the foot of the bed. The shape of Mother's head and shoulders was obvious through the white sheet.

"She looks ridiculous like that," Sue wailed.

"No she doesn't," Julie said violently. Sue reached forward and pulled the sheet clear of Mother's head, and almost simultaneously Julie pinched her hard on the arm and shouted, "Leave it alone." The door behind us opened and Tom was in the room, breathless from his game in the street.

As soon as Julie and I caught hold of him he said, "I want Mum."

"She's asleep," we whispered, "look, you can see." Tom struggled to get by us.

"Why were you shouting then? Anyway, she's not asleep, are you Mum?"

"She's very asleep," said Sue. For a moment it seemed that through sleep, a very deep sleep, we might initiate Tom in the concept of death. But we knew no more about it than he did, and he sensed something was up.

"Mum!" he yelled, and tried to fight his way round the bed. I held him by his wrists.

"You can't," I said. Tom kicked my ankle, pulled free and slipped round Julie to the head of the bed. Steadying himself with one hand on Mother's shoulder, Tom took his shoes off and glared at us triumphantly. Scenes like this had happened before, and sometimes he got his way. By now I was all for letting him find out for himself. I just wanted to watch what happened. But as soon as Tom pulled back the bedclothes to climb in beside his mother, Julie sprang forward and caught Tom by the arm.

"Come on," she said gently, and pulled him.

"No, no . . ." Tom squealed, just as he always did,

and with his free hand held onto the sleeve of Mother's nightdress. As Julie pulled, Mother toppled sideways in a frightening, wooden sort of way, her head struck the bedside table and the clock and the glass of water crashed to the floor. Her head remained wedged between the bed and the table, and now one hand was visible by the pillow. Tom became quiet and still, almost rigid, and let himself be led away like a blindman by Julie. Sue had already left, though I did not notice her go. I paused a moment, wondering whether I should push the corpse into an upright position. I took a pace toward her, but I could not bear the idea of touching her. I ran out of the room, slammed the door shut, turned the key and put it in my pocket.

In the early evening Tom cried himself to sleep on the sofa downstairs. We covered him with a bath towel because no one wanted to go upstairs alone to fetch a blanket. For the rest of the evening we sat about the living room without saying much. Once or twice Sue began to cry, and gave up, as if the effort was too much for her. Julie said, "She probably died in her sleep," and Sue and I nodded.

After a couple of minutes Sue added, "It didn't hurt." Julie and I murmured in agreement.

A long pause and then I said again, "Are you hungry?" My sisters shook their heads. I longed to eat, but I did not want to eat alone. I did not want to do anything alone. When finally they did agree to have something I brought in bread, butter and marmalade and two pints of milk. While we were eating and drinking, conversation picked up. Julie told us that she first "knew" two weeks before my birthday.

"When you did your handstand," I said.

"And you sang 'Greensleeves,'" said Sue, "but what did I do?" We could not remember what Sue had done, and she kept saying, "I know I did *something*," till I told her to shut up. A little after midnight we went upstairs together, keeping very close on the stairs. Julie went first, and I carried Tom. On the first landing we stopped and huddled together before passing Mother's door. I thought I could hear the alarm clock ticking. I was glad the door was locked. We put Tom to bed without waking him. The girls had agreed, without even talking about it, that they would sleep in the same bed. I got into my own bed and lay on my back tensely and turned my head violently to one side whenever there was a thought or an image I wanted to avoid. After half an hour I went into Tom's bedroom and carried him to my own bed. I noticed the light was still on in Julie's room. I put my arms round my brother and fell asleep.


TOWARD THE end of the next day Sue said, "Don't you think we ought to tell someone?"

We were sitting round the rockery. We had spent the whole day in the garden because it was hot and because we were afraid of the house at our backs whose small windows now suggested not concentration, but heavy sleep. In the morning there had been a row over Julie's bikini. Sue thought it was wrong of her to wear it. I said I did not care. Sue said that if Julie wore the bikini it meant "she didn't care about Mum." Tom started to cry and Julie went indoors to take her bikini off. I passed the day looking through a pile of old comics, some of them Tom's. At the back of my mind I had a sense of us sitting about waiting for some terrible event, and then I would remember that it had already happened. Sue looked through her books and sometimes cried to herself. Julie sat on top of the rockery rattling pebbles in her cupped hands, tossing them up and catching them. She was irritable with Tom who one moment was whining and wanting attention, and the next was off playing as if nothing had happened. Once he tried to climb onto Julie's knee and I heard her say as she pushed him away, "Go away. *Please* go away." In the afternoon I read to him from one of the comics.

When Sue asked her question, Julie looked up briefly and looked away. I said, "If we tell someone . . ." and waited.

Sue said, "We have to tell someone so there can be a funeral." I glanced at Julie. She was gazing past our garden fence, across the empty land to the tower blocks.

"If we tell them," I began again, "they'll come and put us into care, into an orphanage or something. They might try and get Tom adopted." I paused. Sue was horrified.

"They can't do that," she said.

"The house will stand empty," I went on, "people will break in, there'll be nothing left."

"But if we don't tell anyone," said Sue, and gestured vaguely toward the house, "what do we do then?"

I looked at Julie again and said louder, "Those kids will come in and smash everything up."

Julie tossed her pebbles across the fence. She said, "We can't leave her in the bedroom or she'll start to smell."

Sue was almost shouting. "That's a terrible thing to say."

"You mean," I said to Julie, "that we shouldn't tell anybody."

Julie walked off toward the house without replying. I watched her go into the kitchen and splash her face at the sink. She held her head under the cold water tap till her hair was soaked; then she wrung it out and swept it clear of her face. As she walked back toward us, drops of water ran onto her shoulders. She sat down on the rockery and said, "If we don't tell anybody we've got to do something ourselves quickly." Sue was close to tears.

"But what can *we* do?" she moaned.

Julie was playing it up a bit. She said very quietly, "Bury her, of course." For all her terseness, her voice still shook.

"Yes," I said, thrilling with horror, "we can have a private funeral, Sue." My younger sister was now weeping steadily, and Julie had her arm round her shoulder. She looked at me coldly over Sue's head. I was suddenly irritated with them both. I got up and walked round to the front of the house to see what Tom was up to.

He was sitting with another boy in the pile of yellow sand by the front gate. They were digging a complicated system of fist-sized tunnels.

"He says," said Tom's friend derisively, squinting up at me, "he says, he says his mum's just died and it's not true."

"It is true," I told him. "She's my mum too, and she's just died."

"Ner-ner, told ya, ner-ner," Tom sneered and plunged his wrists deep into the sand.

His friend thought for a moment. "Well, *my* mum's not dead."

"Don't care," said Tom, working away at his tunnel.

"My mum's not dead," the boy repeated to me.

"So what?" I said.

"Because she isn't," the boy yelled. "She *isn't*." I composed my face and knelt down by them in the sand. I placed my hand sympathetically on the shoulder of Tom's friend.

"I'll tell you something," I said quietly, "I've just come from your house. Your dad told me. Your mum's dead. She came out looking for you and a car run her over."

"Ner-ner, your mum's dead," Tom crowed.

"She isn't," the boy said to himself.

"I'm telling you," I hissed at him, "I've just come from your house. Your dad's pretty upset, and he's really angry with you. Your mum got run over because she was looking for you." The boy stood up. The color had drained from his face. "I wouldn't go home if I was you," I continued, "your dad'll be after you." The boy ran off, up our garden path to the front door. Then he remembered, turned round and ran back. As he passed us he was beginning to blubber.

"Where you going?" Tom shouted after him, but his friend shook his head and kept on running.

As soon as it was dark and we were all indoors,

Tom became fearful and miserable again. He cried when we tried to put him to bed, so we let him stay up and hoped he would fall asleep on the sofa. He whined and cried about the slightest thing, and it was impossible to talk about what we were going to do. We ended up talking round him, shouting over his head. While Tom was screaming and stamping his feet because there was no orange squash left, and Sue was trying to quieten him, I said rapidly to Julie, "Where shall we put her?" She said something, and it was lost to Tom's squeals.

"In the garden, under the rockery," she repeated. Later on Tom cried quite simply for his mother, and while I was trying to comfort him, I saw Julie explaining something to Sue who was nodding her head and rubbing her eyes. As I was attempting to divert Tom with talk of the tunnels he had been building in the sand, I suddenly had my own idea. I lost track of what I was saying, and Tom began to cry loudly once more. He did not fall asleep till after midnight, and only then was I able to tell my sisters that I did not think that the garden was a good plan. We would have to dig deep and it would take a long time. If we did it in the day someone would see us, and if we did it at night we would need torches. We might be seen from the tower blocks. And how would we keep it from Tom? I paused for effect. Despite everything, I was enjoying myself. I had always admired the gentlemen criminals in films who discussed the perfect murder with elegant detachment. As I spoke, I touched the key in my pocket and my stomach turned. I went on confidently, "And of course, if someone came looking, digging up the garden is what they would do first. You read about that sort of thing in the paper every day."

Julie was watching me closely. She appeared to be taking me seriously and when I finished she said, "Well then?"

WE LEFT Sue in the kitchen with Tom. She was not angry or horrified by my idea. She was too miserable to care and shook her head slowly like a sad old lady. Outside there was enough moonlight for us to find the wheelbarrow and a shovel. We pushed it round to the front garden and filled it with sand. We tipped six loads down the coal hole into the cellar, and then we stood outside the kitchen arguing about the water. I said we would have to take it down in buckets. Julie said there was a tap down there. Finally we found it in the small room where all the old clothes and toys were. Because it was farther from the bedroom, the cellar seemed less frightening to me than the rest of the house. Obscurely, I felt entitled to do the shoveling and mixing, but Julie had the shovel and had already made up a pile of sand. She split open one of the cement sacks and stood waiting for me to fetch the water. She worked at great speed, turning and folding the huge pile in on itself till it was a stiff, gray sludge. I lifted the lid of the great tin chest and Julie shoveled the cement in. The cement was now five inches deep on the bottom of the chest. We agreed to do another larger load, and this time I did the mixing and Julie fetched the water. As I worked, the whole purpose of what we were doing never crossed my mind. There was nothing odd about mixing cement. When the second pile of cement was in the chest we had been working three hours. We went upstairs to the kitchen to drink some water. Sue was sleeping in an armchair and Tom lay face down on the sofa. We covered Sue with a coat and returned to the cellar. The chest was now almost half full. We decided that before we fetched her down we should have a really big pile of cement ready. It took us a long time to make this one up. We ran out of sand, and since there was only one shovel, we both went out into the garden again to fetch some more. The sky was already lightening in the east. We made five journeys with the wheelbarrow. I wondered aloud what we would tell Tom when he came out in the morning to find that his sand had disappeared. Julie said, mimicking him, "Blowed away," and we giggled tiredly.

When our final mix was ready it was five o'clock. We had not looked at or spoken to each other for almost an hour. I took the key from my pocket and Julie said, "I thought I'd lost that and you had it all the time."

I followed her up the cellar stairs to the kitchen. We rested and drank some more water. In the living room we pushed some furniture aside and propped open the living-room door with a shoe. Upstairs I was the one who turned the key in the lock and pushed open the door, but it was Julie who stepped into the room first. She was about to turn on the light and then changed her mind. The grayish blue light gave everything in the room a flat, two-dimensional appearance. We seemed to be stepping into an old photograph of Mother's bedroom. I did not look immediately toward the bed. The air was damp and stuffy, as though several people had been sleeping in here with the windows closed. Beyond this closeness was a faint, sharp odor. You could just smell it at the top of your breath, when your lungs were full. I took shallow breaths through my nose. She lay exactly as we had left her, the very image that had been presenting itself whenever I closed my eyes. Julie stood at the foot of the bed hugging herself. I stepped nearer and abandoned the idea that we could ever pick her up. I waited for Julie, but she did not move. I said, "We can't do it." Julie's voice was high-pitched and strained, and she spoke rapidly, as if pretending to be cheerful and efficient.

"We'll wrap her up in the sheet. It won't be so bad. We'll do it quickly, and it won't be so bad." But still she did not move.

I sat down at the table with my back to the bed, and instantly Julie was angry.

"That's right," she said quickly, "leave it to me. Why don't you do something first?"

"Like what?"

"Roll her up in that sheet. It's your plan isn't it?" I wanted to sleep. I closed my eyes and experienced a sharp falling motion. I clutched at the sides of the table and stood up. Julie spoke more gently.

"If we spread the sheet out on the floor, we could lift her onto it." I strode toward my mother and pulled the sheet off her. When I spread the sheet it settled on the floor in such dreamy, slow motion, the corners billowing and folding in on themselves, that I gasped with impatience. I caught my mother by the shoulder, half closed my eyes and pushed her off the table back onto the bed. I avoided her face. She

71

seemed to resist me, and it took both hands to make her move. Now she lay on her side, her arms at odd angles, her body twisted and fixed in the position she had been lying in since the day before yesterday. Julie took her feet and I held her behind her shoulders. When we set her down on the sheet, she looked so frail and sad in her nightdress, lying at our feet like a bird with a broken wing, that for the first time I cried for her and not for myself. Behind her she left on the bed a large brown stain whose outer edges faded to yellow. Julie's face was wet too when we knelt down by Mother and tried to roll her over in the sheet. It was difficult; her body was too twisted to turn.

"She won't go. She won't go," Julie cried in exasperation. At last we succeeded in tucking the sheet round her loosely a couple of times. As soon as she was covered it was a little easier. We picked her up and carried her out of the bedroom.

We brought her down one step at a time, and at the bottom, in the downstairs hall, we rearranged the sheet where it was coming free. My wrists ached. We did not talk about it, but we knew we wanted to get her across the living room without putting her down. We were almost to the kitchen door on the other side when I glanced round to my left, toward Sue's chair. She sat with the coat drawn up to her chin, watching as we passed. I was going to whisper to her but before I could think of anything we were through the kitchen door and edging round to the cellar stairs. We set her down at last several feet away from the trunk. I fetched a bucket of water to moisten our huge pile of cement, and later, when I looked up from the mixing, Sue was standing in the doorway. I thought she might try to stop us, but when Julie and I stood ready to lift the body Sue came and took hold of the middle. Because she would not lie straight, there was barely enough space in the trunk for her. She sank an inch or two into the cement that was already there. I turned for the shovel, but Julie already had it in her hands. As she emptied the first load of wet cement onto Mother's feet, Sue gave out a little cry. And then, as Julie was filling the shovel again, Sue hurried over to the pile, picked up as much cement as she could get in two hands and threw it into the trunk. And then she was throwing cement in as fast as she could. Julie was shoveling faster too, staggering to the trunk with huge loads and running back for more. I plunged my hands into the cement and threw in a heavy armload. We worked like maniacs. Soon only a few patches of the sheet were visible, and then they too were gone. Still we kept on. The only sounds were the scrape of the shovel and our heavy breathing. When we finished, when there was nothing left of the pile but a damp path on the floor, the cement in the trunk was almost overflowing. Before we went back upstairs we stood about looking at what we had done and catching our breath. We decided to leave the lid of the trunk up so the cement would harden quicker.

# Part Two

# Chapter Six

Two or three years before my father died, my parents had to attend the funeral of one of their last surviving relatives. It might have been my mother's aunt, or my father's, or it might have been an uncle. Exactly who had died was not discussed, probably because the death meant very little to our parents. Certainly it meant nothing to us children. We were more interested in the fact that we were to be left alone in the house in charge of Tom for most of the day. Mother prepared us for our responsibilities several days in advance. She would cook our lunch, and all we had to do was warm it up when we were hungry. She showed each one of us in turn, Julie, Sue, then me how to operate the stove and she made us promise to check three times that it was properly turned off. She changed her mind and said she would prepare a cold lunch. But that would not do, she finally decided, because it was winter and we could not go without something hot in the middle of the day. Father, in his turn, told us what to do if someone knocked at the front door, though of course, no one had ever knocked at the front door. He instructed us in what to do if the house caught fire. We were not to stay and fight it, we were to run out of the house to the telephone kiosk and under no circumstances were we to forget Tom. We were not to play down in the cellar, we were not to plug the electric iron in, nor were we to put our fingers in the electric sockets. When we took Tom to the lavatory we were to hold onto him all the time.

We were made to repeat these instructions solemnly till every detail was correct; then we gathered by the front door to watch our parents walk to the bus stop in their black clothes. Every few yards they turned anxiously and waved, and we all waved cheerily back. When they were out of sight Julie slammed the front door shut with her foot, gave out a whoop of delight and in the same movement whipped around and delivered a low, hard punch to my ribs. The blow knocked me back against the wall. Julie ran up the stairs three at a time and looked down at me and laughed. Sue and I flew after her, and upstairs we had a wild, violent pillow fight. Later I made a barricade at the top of the stairs with mattresses and chairs which my sisters stormed from below. Sue filled a balloon with water and threw it at my head. Tom stood at the foot of the stairs, grinning and lurching. An hour later in his excitement he did a shit in his pants, and a rare, sharp smell drifted upstairs and interrupted our fight. Julie and Sue sided. They said I should deal with it because I was the same sex as Tom. I appealed uneasily to the very nature of things and said that, as girls, it was obviously their duty to do something. Nothing was resolved, and our wild battle continued. Soon Tom began to wail. We broke off again. We picked Tom up, carried him to his bedroom and put him in his large brass cot. Julie fetched his harness and tied him down. By now his screams were deafening and his face was a bright pink. We raised the side of the cot and hurried out of the room, anxious to be away from the smell and the screams. Once Tom's bedroom door was shut we could hardly hear a thing, and we carried on our games quite undisturbed.

It was no more than a few hours, but this time seemed to occupy a whole stretch of my childhood. Half an hour before our parents were due back, giggling at the peril we were in, we started to clear up our mess. Between us we cleaned Tom up. We discovered the lunch we had been too busy to eat and tipped it down the lavatory. That evening our shared secret made us delirious. In our pajamas we huddled together in Julie's bedroom and talked of how we would "do it again" soon.

When Mother died, beneath my strongest feelings was a sense of adventure and freedom which I hardly dared admit to myself and which was derived from the memory of that day years ago. But there was no excitement now. The days were too long; it was too hot; the house seemed to have fallen asleep. We did not even sit outside because the wind was blowing a fine, black dust from the direction of the tower blocks and the main roads behind them. And even while it was hot, the sun never quite broke through a high, yellowish cloud; everything I looked at merged and seemed insignificant in the glare. Tom was the only one who was content, in the daytime at least. He had his friend, the one he had played with in the sand. Tom did not seem to notice that the sand was gone, nor did his friend ever mention the story I had given him about his mother. They played farther up the road, in and out of the ruined prefabs. In the evenings, after his friend had gone home, Tom was bad-tempered and cried easily. He went to Julie most often when he wanted attention, and he got on her nerves. "Don't keep asking *me*," she would snap. "Get *away* from me, Tom, just for a minute." But it made little difference. Tom had made up his mind that Julie was to take care of him now. He trailed Julie about the house grizzling, and ignored Sue or me when we tried to divert him. One evening, early on, when Tom was being particularly demanding, and Julie more irritable than usual, she suddenly seized hold of him in the living room and tore his clothes off.

"Right," she kept saying, "you've had it."

"What are you doing?" Sue said over Tom's sobs.

"If he wants to be mothered," Julie shouted, "then he can start doing what I tell him. He's going to bed." It was hardly five o'clock in the afternoon. When Tom was naked, she dragged him by the arm to the bathroom. From there we heard his screams and the sound of bath water running. Ten minutes later Tom was back before us in his pajamas and, utterly subdued, allowed Julie to lead him upstairs to his bedroom. She came down banging imaginary dust from her palms and smiling widely.

"That's what he wanted," she said.

"And that's what you're best at giving," I said. It came out a little more sourly than I intended. Julie kicked my foot gently.

"Watch it," she murmured, "or you'll be next."

As soon as we had finished down in the cellar, Julie and I had gone to bed. Because Sue had slept for some of the night, she stayed up and looked after Tom during the day. I woke in the late afternoon extremely thirsty and hot. There was no one downstairs, but I could hear Tom's voice somewhere outside. As I stooped to drink water from the kitchen tap a cloud of flies hummed around my face. I walked on the sides of my bare feet because the floor around the sink was covered with something yellow and sticky, probably spilled orange juice. Still light-headed from my sleep, I went upstairs to Sue's room. She was sitting across her bed with her back against the wall. Her knees were drawn up and in her lap was an open notebook. She put down her pencil when I came in and snapped the book shut. It was stuffy as if she had been in here for hours. I sat down on the edge of her bed, quite near her. I felt like talking, but not about the night before. I wanted someone to stroke my head. Sue pressed her thin lips together, as though determined not to speak first.

"What are you doing?" I said at last, and stared at the notebook.

"Nothing," she said, "just writing." She held her notebook in two hands against her belly.

"What are you writing?"

She sighed. "Nothing. Just writing." I tore the book from her hands, turned my back on her and opened it. Before she blocked my view with her arm I had time to read at the top of a page, "Tuesday, Dear Mum."

"Give it back," Sue shouted, and her voice was so unfamiliar, so unexpectedly violent, that I let her take it from me. She put the book under her pillow and sat on the edge of the bed, staring at the wall in front of her. She was red in the face, and her freckles were darker. The pulse in her temple stood out and beat angrily. I shrugged and decided to leave, but she did not look up. When I was through the door, she pushed it shut and locked it, and as I was walking away, I heard her crying. I knocked on her door and called to her. Through her sobs she told me to go away, and that was what I did. I went to the bathroom and washed the dried cement from my hands.

For a week after the burial we did not eat a cooked meal. Julie went to the post office for money and came home with bags of shopping, but the vegetables and meat she bought lay around untouched until they had to be thrown away. Instead we ate bread, cheese, peanut butter, biscuits and fruit. Tom gorged himself on bars of chocolate and did not seem to need much else. When someone felt like making it, we drank tea, but mostly we had water from the kitchen tap. The day Julie bought the shopping, she gave Sue and me two pounds each.

"How much are you getting then?" I asked her. She snapped her purse shut.

"Same as you," she said. "The rest is for food and stuff."

It was not long before the kitchen was a place of stench and clouds of flies. None of us felt like doing anything about it beyond keeping the kitchen door shut. It was too hot. Then someone, not me, threw the meat out. Encouraged, I cleaned out some milk bottles, gathered up empty wrappers and swatted a dozen or so of the flies. That same night Julie told Sue and me it was time we did something about the kitchen. I said, "I did a lot of things in there today which you two don't seem to have noticed."

The girls laughed.

"Like what?" Sue said, and when I told them, they laughed again, louder than they needed to.

"Oh well," they said to each other. "He's done his bit for a few weeks."

I decided then to have nothing more to do with the kitchen, and this made Julie and Sue determined not to clean it up either. It was not until we cooked a meal, several days later, that something was finally done. In the meantime the flies spread through the house and hung in thin clouds by the windows and made a constant clicking sound as they threw themselves against the glass.

I masturbated each morning and afternoon and drifted through the house, from one room to another, sometimes surprised to find myself in my bedroom, lying on my back, staring at the ceiling, when I had intended to go out into the garden. I looked at myself carefully in the mirror. What was wrong with me? I tried to frighten myself with the reflection of my eyes, but I felt only impatience and mild revulsion. I stood in the center of my room listening to the very distant, constant sound of traffic. Then I listened to the voices of children playing in the street. The two sounds merged and seemed to press down on the top of my head. I lay on the bed again and this time I closed my eyes. When a fly walked across my face I was determined not to move. I could not bear to remain on the bed, and yet any activity I thought of disgusted me in advance. To stir myself I thought of my mother downstairs. She was no more to me than a fact. I got up and went to the window and stood several minutes, looking out across the parched weeds to the tower blocks. Then I looked through the house to see if Julie was back; she frequently disappeared, usually in the afternoons and for hours on end. When I asked her where she went, she told me to mind my own business. Julie was not in, and Sue had locked herself in her room. If I knocked on her door she would ask me what I wanted, and I would not know what to tell her. I remembered the two pounds. I left the house by the back and climbed over the fence so that Tom would not see me and want to come with me. For no particular reason at all I set off at a run toward the shops.

I had no idea what I wanted. I thought I would know when I saw it, and even if it cost more than two pounds, then at least I would have something to want, something to think about. I ran all the way. The main shopping street was empty except for cars. It was Sunday. The only person I could see was a woman in a red coat standing on a footbridge that spanned the road. I wondered why she wore a red coat in such heat. Perhaps she was wondering why I had been running for she seemed to be staring in my direction. She was still a long way off, but she looked familiar. She could have been a teacher at my school. I walked toward the footbridge because I did not want to turn back so soon. As I walked I stared into the shop windows on my left. I did not like meeting schoolteachers in the street. I thought I could pass beneath her, if she was still there, and pretend I had not seen her. But fifty yards from the bridge I could not resist glancing up. The woman was my mother, and she was looking right at me. I stopped. She had shifted her weight from one foot to the other, but she did not move from her position. I started toward her again. I found it was difficult to make my legs move and my heart beat so fast I was certain I would be sick. When I was almost under the footbridge I stopped again and looked up. Great relief and recognition swept through me and I laughed out loud. It was not Mother, of course; it was Julie, wearing a coat I had never seen before.

"Julie!" I called up. "I thought you...." I ran under the bridge and up a flight of wooden stairs. Face to face with her now I saw that it was not Julie either. She had a thin face and straggling grayish black hair. I could not tell if she was young or old. She put her hands deep into her pockets and swayed slightly.

"I ain't got any money," she said, "so don't you come near me."

As I walked home my blankness returned, and significance drained from the event of my day. I went straight upstairs to my bedroom, and although I did not meet or hear anyone, I knew the others were in. I took off all my clothes and lay under the

sheet on my bed. Sometime later I was woken from
a heavy sleep by the sound of shrill laughter. I was
curious, but for some reason I did not move at first.
I preferred to listen. The voices were Julie's and
Sue's. At the end of each burst of laughter they
made a sighing, singing sound which merged into
words I could not make out. Then the laughter
began again. I felt irritable after my sudden sleep.
My head felt tight and shrunken; the objects in the
room seemed too dense, locked hard into the space
they occupied and bulging with strain. My clothes,
before I picked them up and put them on, could
have been made of steel. When I was dressed I stood
outside my bedroom listening. I heard only the
murmur of one voice and the creak of a chair. I went
down the stairs as quietly as possible. I had a strong
wish to spy on my sisters, to be with them and be
invisible. It was completely dark in the large
hallway, downstairs. I was able to stand a little back
from the open living-room door without being seen.
Sue I could see clearly; she was sitting at the table,
cutting something with a large pair of scissors. Julie,
who was partly obscured by the doorframe, stood
with her back to me and I could not see what she was
doing. Her arm moved forward and back with a
faint, rasping sound. Just as I was moving to see
better a little girl stepped in front of Julie and went
to stand by Sue's elbow. Julie turned also and stood
behind the girl, one hand resting on her shoulder. In
her other hand she held a hairbrush. They remained
grouped like this for a while without talking. When
Sue turned a little, I saw she was cutting blue cloth.
The little girl leaned backward against Julie who
clasped her hands under the girl's chin and tapped
her gently on the chest with the brush.

Of course, as soon as the girl spoke I knew it was Tom. He said, "It takes a long time, doesn't it?" and Sue nodded. I took a couple of paces into the room and was not noticed. Tom and Julie were intent on watching Sue who was making alterations to one of her school skirts. She had cut it shorter, and now she was beginning to sew. Tom was wearing an orange-colored dress that looked familiar, and from somewhere they had found him a wig. His hair was fair and thick with curls. How easy it was to be someone else. I crossed my arms and hugged myself. They are only clothes and a wig, I thought, it is Tom dressed up. But I was looking at another person, someone who could expect a life quite different from Tom's. I was excited and scared. I squeezed my hands together and the movement caused all three to turn and look at me.

"What are you doing?" I said after a pause.

"Dressing him up," Sue said and turned back to her sewing.

Tom glanced at me, half turned toward the table where Sue was working and stared fixedly into one corner of the room. He played with the hem of his dress, rolling the material between his forefinger and thumb.

"What's the point of it?" I said.

Julie shrugged and smiled. She wore faded jeans rolled up above her knees and an unbuttoned shirt over her bikini top. She had tied a piece of blue ribbon in her hair and she held another piece in her hand, wound around her finger.

Julie came and stood right in front of me. "Oh come on," she said, "cheer up, misery." She smelled sweetly of her suntan oil, and I could feel the warmth her skin gave off. She must have been out in the sun all day, somewhere. She unwound the ribbon from her finger and draped it round my neck. I pushed her hands away when she started to tie a bow under my chin but I did it without conviction and she persisted and finished the knot. She took my hand and I followed my sister to the table. "Here's another one," she said to Sue, "who's tired of being a grumpy boy." I would have untied the ribbon but I did not wish to let go of Julie's hand which was dry and cool. Now we all watched over Sue's shoulder. I had never realized how skillful she was at sewing. Her hand flew backward and forward in the same regular motion like a shuttle on a mechanical loom. And yet her actual progress was slow, and I felt great impatience. I wanted to sweep the cloth, needle and pins to the floor in one movement. We would have to wait till she finished before we could speak or before anything else could happen.

Finally she broke the cotton with a sharp tug of her wrists and stood up. Julie let go of my hand and stood behind Tom. He raised his hands and she lifted the dress over his head. Underneath he was wearing his own white shirt. Sue helped Tom into the blue pleated skirt and Julie knotted one of Sue's school ties around his neck. I watched and fingered my blue ribbon. If I took it off now I would become a spectator again, I would have to decide on an attitude toward what was going on. Tom put on white socks and Sue fetched her beret. The girls laughed and chatted while these preparations were being made. Sue was telling Julie a story about a friend at school who had her hair cut very short. She came into school in trousers and went into the boys' changing room and saw them all at the urinals. She burst out laughing at the sight of the whole row of them and gave herself away.

"Isn't he pretty?" Julie said. While we gazed at him, Tom stood perfectly still with his hands behind his back and his eyes lowered. If he enjoyed being dressed up he didn't really show it. He went out into the hallway to admire himself in the full-length mirror. I watched him through the doorway. He stood sideways to his reflection and stared at himself over his shoulder.

While Tom was out of the room Julie took both my hands in hers and said, "Now what are we going to do with grumpy?" Julie's eyes roved over my face. "You won't make a pretty girl like Tom with horrible spots like those."

Sue, who now stood at my elbow tugged at a strand of my hair and said, "Or with long greasy hair he never washes."

"Or with yellow teeth," said Julie.

"Or smelly feet," said Sue. Julie turned my hands so the palms faced down.

"Or with filthy fingernails." The girls pored over my fingernails, making exaggerated sounds of disgust. Tom watched from the door. I was rather enjoying myself, standing there being examined.

"Look at that one," Sue said, and I felt her touch my forefinger. "It's got green *and* red under it." They laughed; they seemed to take great delight in everything they found.

"What's that?" I said, looking across the room. Almost concealed under a chair was a long cardboard box with its lid half off. White tissue paper spilled out from one corner.

"Ah!" Sue cried. "That's Julie's."

I strode across the room and pulled the box clear of the chair. Inside, embedded in white and orange tissue was a pair of calf-length boots. They were deep brown and gave off a rich smell of leather and perfume.

With her back to me Julie was slowly and carefully folding the orange dress Tom had worn. I held up one of the boots.

"Where did you get these?"

"In a shop," Julie said without turning round.

"How much?"

"Not much."

Sue was very excited. "Julie!" She said in a very loud whisper, "They cost thirty-eight pounds."

I said, "You paid thirty-eight pounds?"

Julie shook her head and put the orange dress under her arm. I remembered the ridiculous ribbon around my neck and tried to yank it free, but it would not come; the bow turned into a knot. Sue started to laugh. Julie was walking out of the room.

"You nicked them," I said, and again she shook her head. Still holding the boot in my hand, I followed her up the stairs. When we were in her bedroom I said, "You gave me and Sue two quid each and then you spent thirty-eight pounds on a pair of boots." Julie had sat down in front of a mirror she had fixed against the wall and was running a brush through her hair.

"Wrong," she said in a chiming voice, as if we were playing a guessing game. I threw the boot on the bed and used two hands to break the ribbon round my neck. The knot grew smaller and hard like a stone. Julie stretched her arms and yawned.

"If you didn't buy them," I said, "then you must have nicked them."

She said, "Nope," and kept her mouth pursed round the word in a kind of mocking smile.

"What then?" I stood right behind her. She was looking at herself in the mirror, not at me.

"Can't you think of another way?"

I shook my head.

"There isn't another way, unless you made them yourself."

Julie laughed.

"Hasn't anyone ever given you a present?"

"Who gave them to you?"

"A friend."

"Who though?"

"Aha, that would be telling."

"A bloke."

Julie stood up and turned round to look at me and made her lips small and tight like a berry.

"Of course he's a bloke," she said at last. I had a confused notion that as Julie's brother I had a right to ask questions about her boyfriend. But there was nothing about Julie to support such an idea, and I felt more dejected than curious. She picked up a pair of nail scissors from her bedside table and cut through the ribbon close to the knot. As she pulled it clear and let it fall to the floor she said, "There," and kissed me lightly on my mouth.

# Chapter Seven

THREE WEEKS after Mother died I began to reread the book Sue had given me for my birthday. I was surprised how much I had missed. I never noticed how particular Commander Hunt was about keeping the ship clean and tidy, especially on the really long journeys through space. Each day, the old earth day, he climbed down a stainless steel ladder and inspected the messroom. Cigarette ends, plastic cutlery, old magazines, coffee cups and spilled coffee hung untidily about the room. "Now that we do not have gravity to keep things in their place," Commander Hunt told the computer technicians who were new to space travel, "we must make an extra effort to be neat." And during the long hours when there were no urgent decisions to be taken, Commander Hunt passed the time "reading and rereading the masterpieces of world literature, and writing down his thoughts in a massive steel-bound journal while Cosmo, his faithful hound, dozed at his feet." Commander Hunt's space ship sped across the universe at one-hundredth the speed of light in search of the source of energy that had transformed the spores into a monster. I wondered if he would have cared about the state of the messroom, or about world literature, if the ship had remained perfectly still, fixed in outer space.

As soon as I had finished the book I took it downstairs to give to Julie or Sue. I wanted someone else to read it. I found Julie alone in the living room sitting in an armchair with her feet tucked under her. She was smoking a cigarette, and as I came into the room she tilted her head back and blew a column of smoke toward the ceiling. I said, "I didn't know you smoked." She took another drag and nodded curtly. I approached her with the book. "You should read this," I said, and put it in her hand.

Julie spent some time staring at the cover, and I stood behind her chair looking at the monster attacking the spaceship. In the distance Commander Hunt's ship was racing to the rescue. I had not examined the cover closely before, and now it looked ridiculous. I felt ashamed of it, as if I had painted it myself. Julie handed the book to me over her shoulder. She held it by one corner.

"The cover's not much," I said, "but it's got some really good things." Julie shook her head and blew out more smoke, this time straight across the room.

"It's not my sort of book," she said. I placed the book on the table face down and walked round to the front of Julie's chair.

"What do you mean?" I said. "How do you know what sort of book it is?"

Julie shrugged.

"I don't feel much like reading anyway."

"You would if you started reading this." I picked up the book again and stared at it. I did not know why I was so anxious to have someone else read it. Suddenly Julie leaned forward and took the book out of my hand.

"All right," she said, "if you really want me to, I'll read it." She spoke as if to a child about to burst into tears.

I was angry. I said, "Don't read it just to please me," and tried to take it back from her. She moved the book out of my reach.

"Oh no," she said through a smile, "of course not." I grabbed her wrist and twisted it back. Julie transferred the book to her other hand and slipped it under her backside. "You're hurting me."

"Give it back," I said, "it's not your sort of book." I pulled her sideways so that the book was revealed. She let me have it without any further struggle, and I took it to the far side of the room. Julie stared at me and rubbed her wrist.

"What's wrong with you?" she said almost in a whisper. "You ought to be locked up." I ignored her and sat down.

We sat in silence on opposite sides of the room for a long time. Julie lit another cigarette and I looked at certain passages in my book. My eyes moved across the lines of print but I was taking nothing in. I wished to say something conciliatory to Julie before I left the room. But I could think of nothing that did not sound stupid. And besides, I told myself, she had asked for it. The day before I had made Tom cry by flicking his head with my fingernail. He had been making a row outside my bedroom door and had woken me up. He lay on the floor, clutching his head and screamed so loud that Sue came running out of her bedroom.

"It's his own fault," I said, "making a noise like that first thing in the morning." Sue rubbed Tom's head.

"First thing!" she said loudly over Tom's screams. "It's almost one o'clock."

"Well it's still first thing in the morning for me," I shouted and went back to bed.

As far as I was concerned, there was not much point in getting up. There was nothing particularly interesting to eat, and I was the only one with nothing to do. Tom played outside all day, Sue stayed in her room reading books and writing in her notebook, and Julie went out with whoever gave her the boots. When she was not out she was getting ready. She took long baths which filled the house with a sweet smell, stronger than the smell from the kitchen. She spent a long time washing and brushing her hair and doing things to her eyes. She wore clothes I had never seen before, a silk blouse and a brown velvet skirt. I woke in the late morning, masturbated and dozed off again. I had dreams, not exactly nightmares, but bad dreams that I struggled to wake out of. I spent my two pounds on fish and chips, and when I asked Julie for more she handed over a fiver without a word. During the day I listened to the radio. I thought about returning to school at the end of the summer, and I thought about getting a job. I was not drawn to either of these. Some afternoons I fell asleep in the armchair even though I had only been awake a couple of hours. I looked in the mirror and saw that the spots on my face were spreading down the sides of my neck. I wondered if they would cover my whole body, and I did not much care if they did.

Finally Julie cleared her throat and said, "Well?" I looked past her at the kitchen door.

"Let's clean up the kitchen," I said suddenly. It was exactly the right thing to say. Julie stood up immediately and did an imitation of a film gangster, cigarette butt dangling from one corner of her mouth.

"Now you're talking, brother, really talking." She offered me her hand and pulled me out of my chair.

"I'll get Sue," I said, but Julie shook her head.

With an imaginary Sten gun at her hip she leaped into the kitchen and shot the place apart, all the mold-covered plates, the flies and bluebottles, the huge pile of rubbish that had collapsed and spread across the floor. Julie shot it all, with the same stuttering noises from the back of her throat that Tom used in his gun games. I stood by wondering whether I should join in this game. Julie whipped round and filled my belly with her bullets. I collapsed on the floor at her feet, a butter wrapper inches from my nose. Julie took a handful of my hair and pulled my head back. She swapped her gun for a knife, and as she pressed it against my throat she said, "Any more trouble and I'll stick it in here." Then she knelt down and pressed her fist near my groin. "Or here," she whispered dramatically, and we both laughed.

Julie's game was over very suddenly. We began to sweep up the rubbish and stuff it into cardboard boxes which we carried out to the dustbins. Sue heard us and came down to help. We unblocked the drains, washed the walls and scrubbed the floor. While Sue and I washed the dishes, Julie went out to buy food for a meal. We finished just as she returned, and we began cutting up vegetables for a large stew. Once that was simmering Julie and Sue tidied up the living room and I went outside to clean the windows. I saw my sisters, blurred by a film of water, moving all the furniture into the center of the room and for the first time in weeks I was happy. I felt safe, as if I belonged to a powerful, secret army. We worked for over four hours and I was hardly aware of my existence.

I took some mats and a small carpet into the garden and thrashed the dust out of them with a stick. I was well into this when I heard a sound behind me and turned round. It was Tom and his friend from the tower block. Tom was wearing Sue's school uniform and his knees were bloody from a fall. Quite often now Tom played in the street in Sue's skirt. None of the other children teased him as I thought they would. They did not even seem to notice. I could not understand that. I would not have been seen dead in my sister's skirt at Tom's age, or any age. He stood holding his friend's hand and I went on with my work. Round his neck Tom's friend wore a scarf, the pattern of which was familiar to me. They had a short conversation which I could not hear above the noise I was making. Then Tom said loudly, "What are you doing that for?"

I told him and said, "Why are you wearing a skirt?" Tom did not reply. I hit the carpet a few more times and then I stopped again and said to Tom's friend, "Why is Tom wearing a skirt?"

"In our game," he said, "Tom is being Julie."

I said, "And who are you?"

The boy did not reply.

I raised the stick and just as I was bringing it down Tom said, "He's being you."

"Did you say me?" They both nodded. I threw the stick away and pulled the mats off the clothesline. I said, "What do you do in your game?"

Tom's friend shrugged. "Nothing much."

"Do you have fights?" I tried to include Tom in my question but he was looking in another direction. The other boy shook his head. I laid the mats and the carpet on top of each other. "Are you friends in your game? Do you hold hands?" They pulled their hands free and laughed.

Tom followed me into the house, but his friend remained outside the kitchen door. He called out to Tom, "I'm going home," and made it sound like a question. Tom nodded without turning round. In the living room there were four plates on the table, and on either side of each plate was a knife and fork. In the center of the table there was a bottle of tomato sauce and an eggcup full of salt. There was a chair for each plate. I thought, As if we were real people. Tom went upstairs to see Julie, and Sue and I walked backward and forward between the kitchen and the living room like Commander Hunt inspecting the messroom. Twice I bent down and picked pieces of fluff off the carpet. On a hook that was fixed onto the cellar door was a shopping bag made of brightly colored string. At the bottom of the bag were two apples and two oranges. I pushed the bag with my finger and made it swing like a pendulum. It moved more freely in one direction than in the other, and it took me a while to discover that this was because of the shape of the handles on the bag. Without thinking I pulled the cellar door open, turned on the light and ran down the stairs.

The shovel lay in the center of a large, round stain of dried cement. It made me think of the hour hand of a big broken clock. I tried to think which of us had used it last, but now I had no clear memory of the order of events. I picked it up and leaned it against the wall. The lid of the trunk was open, the way we had left it. I could remember that. I ran my hand across the concrete that filled the trunk. It was a very pale gray, and it felt warm to touch. A fine dust rubbed onto my hand. I noticed that running diagonally across the surface was a hairline crack which forked at one end. I knelt down and put my nose to it and sniffed. There was a very distinct sweet smell, but when I stood up again I realized I had smelled the stew cooking upstairs. I sat down on a stool by the trunk and thought about my mother. I tried hard to make a picture of her face in my mind. I had the oval outline of a face, but the features inside this shape would not stay still, or they dissolved into each other and the oval turned into a light bulb. When I closed my eyes I actually saw a light bulb. Once my mother's face appeared briefly framed by the oval and smiling unnaturally the way she did when she posed for snapshots. I made up sentences and tried to make her say them. But there was nothing I could imagine her saying. The simplest things like "pass me that book" or "good night" did not sound like the kinds of things she would say. Was her voice low or high? Had she ever made a joke? She had been dead less than a month, and she was in the trunk beside me. Even that was not certain. I wanted to dig her out and see.

I ran my fingernail along the fine crack. It was not at all clear to me now why we had put her in the trunk in the first place. At the time it had been obvious, to keep the family together. Was that a good reason? It might have been more interesting to be apart. Nor could I think whether what we had done was an ordinary thing to do, understandable even if it had been a mistake. Just like my picture of her face, every thought I had dissolved into nothing.

The impossibility of knowing or feeling anything for certain gave me a great urge to masturbate. I put my hands into my pants, and as I glanced down between my legs, I saw something red. I leaped up in astonishment. The stool I was sitting on was bright red. It had been painted long ago by my father and it belonged in the downstairs bathroom. Julie or Sue must have brought it down in order to sit by the trunk. Instead of being a comforting idea, it frightened me. We hardly spoke at all to each other about Mother. She was everyone's secret. Even Tom rarely mentioned her and only occasionally cried for her now. I looked around the cellar for other signs, but there was nothing. I left, and when I started up the steps I saw Sue standing at the top watching me.

"I thought that was you down there," she said when I reached her. She had a plate in her hand.

I said, "There's a crack, did you see it?"

"It's getting bigger," she said quickly, "but guess what?" I shrugged. She showed me the plate.

"Someone's coming to tea."

I pushed past her into the kitchen but there was no one there. Sue turned out the cellar light and locked the door.

"Who?" I could see now that Sue was very excited.

"Derek," she said, "Julie's bloke."

In the living room I watched her set the extra place. She took me to the foot of the stairs, pointed upward and whispered, "Listen." I heard Julie's voice and then, in answer, a man's voice. Suddenly both talked at once and both laughed.

"So what?" I said to Sue. "Big deal."

My heart was racing. I lay across an armchair and started to whistle. Sue came and sat down too and wiped imaginary sweat from her brow.

"It's lucky we cleaned up, isn't it?"

I went on whistling, choosing my notes at random, in a kind of panic, and only gradually settling on a tune.

Tom came in from upstairs carrying in his arms what looked like a large cat. It was his wig. He carried it to Sue and asked her to put it on him. She held him away from her and pointed at his knees and hands. She refused to let him have the wig until he had washed.

While Tom was in the bathroom I said, "What's he like?"

"He's got a car, a new one, look," and she pointed toward the window. But I did not look round.

When Tom returned to Sue she said, "If you want to be a girl at tea, why don't you wear the orange dress?"

He shook his head, and Sue fitted the wig. He ran into the hall to look in the mirror and then sat down opposite me and picked his nose. Sue was reading a book and I began to whistle again, this time more softly. Tom brought something from his nose on the end of his forefinger, glanced at it and wiped it on a chair cushion. I sometimes did that myself, but only when alone, usually in bed in the morning. It doesn't look so bad when a little girl does it, I thought, and went to the window. It was a sports car, the old-fashioned kind with a running board and a leather hood that was folded back. It was bright red with a thin black line running its whole length.

"You should go out and look at it," Sue said, "it's fantastic."

"Look at what?" I said. The wheels had silver spokes, and the exhaust pipes were silver too. Along the side of the hood were long, slanting cuts in the metal. "To let the air in," I heard myself explain to a passenger, and swung the machine through a tight bend in the Alps, "or the heat out." When I went back to my chair Sue had disappeared.

I stared at Tom. In the large armchair he looked tiny, for his feet only just stuck out over the edge of the seat and his head came halfway up the backrest. He stared back at me for a few seconds; then he looked away and folded his arms. His legs splayed out from under his skirt.

I said, "What's it like being a girl?" Tom shook his head and shifted his position. "Is it better than being a boy?"

"Dunno."

"Does it make you feel sexy?"

Tom laughed suddenly. He did not understand what I meant, but he knew the word was a signal to laugh.

"Well, does it?" He grinned at me.

"I dunno."

I leaned forward and wiggled my finger at him to make him come closer.

"When you put your wig on and the skirt, and then you go to the mirror and see a little girl, do you get a nice feeling in your dinky, does it get bigger?"

Tom's grin faded away. He climbed off the armchair and slipped out of the room. I remained perfectly still, aware of the smell of the stew. The ceiling creaked. I arranged myself in my chair. I crossed my legs at the ankles and clasped my hands together under my chin. There were light, fast footsteps on the stairs and Tom came running in.

"They're coming! He's coming!" he said loudly.

I said, "Who is?" and moved my hands behind my head.

Julie said, "This is Derek. This is Jack."

I shook hands without standing up but I uncrossed my legs and put my feet firmly on the floor. Neither of us spoke as we shook hands. Afterward Derek cleared his throat and looked at Julie. She was standing right behind Tom with her hands pressing down on his shoulders. She said, "This is Tom," in a way that made it obvious she had already spoken to Derek about him.

Derek moved behind my chair where I could not see him and said quietly, "Ah, a tomgirl." Sue made a half-hearted sort of laugh, and I stood up. Julie went into the kitchen to fetch the stew and called to Tom to help her. The three of us stood in the center of the room. We were rather close and we seemed to sway a little together. Sue deliberately made her voice breathless and stupid.

"We really like your car." Derek nodded. He was very tall and looked as if he were dressed for a wedding—pale gray suit, cream-colored shirt and tie, cuff links and a waistcoat with a small silver chain.

I said, "I don't like it much."

He turned to me and smiled faintly. He had a thick black mustache. It looked so perfect that it could have been made of plastic.

"Oh?" he said politely through his smile. "Why not?"

"It's too flash," I said. Derek glanced down at his shoes, and I went on. "I mean the color, I don't like red."

"Too bad," he said, looking at Sue, not me. "Do *you* like red?" Sue looked over Derek's shoulder into the kitchen.

"Me? Oh, I like red, especially on cars."

Now that he was looking at me again I repeated, "I don't like red on cars. It makes them look like toys."

Derek took a step away from both of us. Both his hands were deep in his pockets and he rocked back on his heels. He spoke very quietly.

"When you're a bit older you'll realize that's all they are, toys, expensive toys."

"Why are they toys?" I said. "They're very useful for getting about." He nodded and looked all around the room.

"These are big rooms," he said to Sue, "it's a really big house."

Sue said, "My room's quite small." I folded my arms and persisted.

"If cars are toys, then everything you buy is a toy."

Just then Julie came in with the stew, followed by Tom carrying a loaf of bread and a pepper pot.

"I'll have to think about that one, Jack," Derek said, and turned to move a chair out of Julie's way.

Before we sat down I noticed that Julie was wearing her new boots and the velvet skirt and the silk blouse. She and Derek sat next to each other at the table. I sat at a corner next to Tom. At first I was too irritated to feel hungry. When Julie passed me a plate of food I told her I didn't want it. She said, "Don't be silly," put the plate down between my knife and fork and smiled at Derek. He nodded, understanding everything. While we ate Julie and Sue did all the talking. Derek sat perfectly upright. He spread a red and blue handkerchief over his lap and when he had finished he dabbed at his mustache with it. Then he folded it up carefully before he put it in his pocket. I wanted to see them touch each other. Julie rested her head on the crook of his elbow and asked for the salt to be passed. I reached the eggcup before Derek, and as I snatched it across to my sister salt spilled the length of the table.

"Careful," Derek said softly. The girls began a jumpy conversation about throwing salt over your shoulder and walking under ladders. At one point I saw Derek wink at Tom who lowered his head so his curls hid his face.

Afterward Julie took Derek out into the garden, and Sue and I washed the dishes. I did no more than stand about with a dishcloth in my hand. We watched out the kitchen window. Julie was pointing to the little paths and steps which were now almost invisible under the tangle of brownish weeds. Derek pointed toward the tower blocks and made a wide sweep with his arm as if ordering them to collapse. Julie was nodding seriously.

Sue said, "He's got really broad shoulders, hasn't he? He must have had that suit made specially."

We stared at Derek's back. His head was small and round, the hair all the same length, like a brush.

"He's not so strong," I said, "and he's pretty thick." Sue lifted wet plates out of the sink and looked for somewhere to put them.

"He could beat you up with his little finger," she said.

"Hah!" I cried. "Let him try it."

A little later Julie and her boyfriend sat down by the rockery. Sue took the cloth from me and started to dry the dishes. She said, "I bet you can't guess what he does," and I answered, "I don't give a fuck what he does."

"You'll never guess. He's a snooker player."

"So what?"

"He plays snooker for money; he's incredibly rich."

I looked at Derek again and thought about this. He was sitting sideways to me listening to Julie. He had pulled up a long stalk of grass and he was biting small pieces off it and spitting them out. All the time he nodded at what Julie was saying, and when at last he spoke he rested his hand lightly on her shoulder. What he said made Julie laugh.

"And there was something about him in the paper," Sue was saying.

"What paper?"

Sue named the local weekly and I laughed.

"Everyone gets written about in that," I said, "if they live long enough."

"I bet you don't know how old he is." I made no reply. "Twenty-three," Sue said proudly and smiled at me. I wanted to hit her.

"What's so amazing about that?"

Sue dried her hands. "It's a perfect age for a bloke."

I said, "What are you talking about? Who said?"

Sue hesitated. "Julie said."

I gasped and ran out of the kitchen. In the living room I paused to look for Commander Hunt. He had been tidied away into a bookshelf. I ran upstairs with the book to the bedroom, slammed the door hard and lay down on the bed.

# Chapter Eight

MORE FREQUENTLY my bad dreams became nightmares. There was a huge wooden box in the hallway
which I must have passed a dozen times before
without giving it a second thought. Now I stopped
to look. The lid that used to be nailed on tight was
hanging loose, some of the nails were bent back and
the wood around them was splintered and white. I
was standing as near to the box as I could without
being able to see inside. I knew I was in a dream and
that it was important not to panic. Something was
in the box. I managed to open my eyes a little and
saw the bottom corner of my bed before they
weighed shut. I was in the hallway again, a little
closer to the box and foolishly peering in. When I

tried my eyes again they opened easily and wide. I saw the corner of my bed and some of my clothes. In a large armchair at the side of my bed sat my mother, staring at me with huge, hollow eyes. That's because she's dead, I thought. She was tiny and her feet hardly touched the floor. When she spoke her voice was so familiar that I could not imagine how I could have forgotten it so easily. But I could not understand exactly what she was saying. She used a strange word, "drubbing" or "brudding."

"Can't you stop drubbing," she said, "even while I'm talking to you?"

"I'm not doing anything," I said, and noticed as I glanced down that there were no clothes on the bed and that I was naked and masturbating in front of her. My hand flew backward and forward like a shuttle on a loom. I told her, "I can't stop, it's nothing to do with me."

"What would your father say," she said sadly, "if he was alive?"

As I woke up I was saying out loud, "But you're both dead."

I told this dream to Sue one afternoon. When she unlocked her door to let me in I noticed that she held her notebook open in one hand. While she was listening to me she closed it and slid it under her pillow. To my surprise my dream made her giggle.

"Do boys do that all the time?" she said.

"Do what?"

"You know, drubbing."

Instead of answering her I said, "Do you remember when we used to play that game?"

"What game?"

110

"When Julie and I were the doctors examining you, and you were from another planet."

My sister nodded and folded her arms. I paused. I had no idea what it was I was going to say.

"Well, what about it?" I had come to talk about my dream and about Mother, and already we were talking about something else.

"Don't you wish," I said slowly, "that we still played that game?" Sue shook her head and looked away.

"I can hardly remember anything about it."

"Julie and I used to take all your clothes off." It sounded unlikely as I said it.

Sue shook her head again and said unconvincingly, "Did you? I don't really remember it that well, I wasn't very old." Then, after a silence, she added warmly, "We were always playing silly games."

I sat down on Sue's bed. The floor of her bedroom was covered with books, some of them open and placed face downward. Many of them were from the library and I was about to pick one up when I felt suddenly weary of the whole idea of books. I said, "Don't you ever get tired of sitting in here all day reading?"

"I like reading," Sue said, "and there's nothing else to do."

I said, "There's all kinds of things to do," simply to hear Sue say again that there was nothing to do.

But she sucked her thin pale lips into her mouth, the way women do after they put lipstick on their lips, and said, "I don't feel like doing anything else."

After this we sat in silence for rather a long time.

Sue whistled, and I sensed she was waiting for me to leave. We heard the back door open downstairs and the voices of Julie and her boyfriend. I wished that Sue disliked Derek the way I did; then we could have all sorts of things to talk about. She raised her faint eyebrows and said, "That will be them," and I said, "So?" and felt isolated from everyone I knew.

Sue resumed her whistling and I turned the pages of a magazine, but we were both listening carefully. They were not coming upstairs. I heard the sound of running water and the rattle of teacups. I said to Sue, "But you still write in that book, don't you?"

She said, "A bit," and looked toward her pillow as if she was prepared to stop me snatching it.

I waited a moment, and then I said in a very sad voice, "I wish you'd let me see the bits about Mum, just those bits. You could read them to me if you like." Downstairs the radio came on at full volume. *"If you ever plan to motor west, take my way, that's the highway that's the best. . . ."* The song irritated me but I remained looking sadly at my sister.

"You wouldn't understand any of it."

"Why not?"

Sue spoke quickly. "You never understood anything about her. You were always horrible to her."

"That's a lie," I said loudly, and after a few seconds I repeated, "That's a lie." Sue sat on the edge of her bed, her back straight and one hand resting on the pillow. When she spoke she stared mournfully in front of her.

"You never did anything she asked you. You never did anything to help. You were always too full of yourself, just like you are now."

I said, "I wouldn't have dreamed about her like that if I didn't care about her."

"You didn't dream about her," Sue said, "you dreamed about yourself. That's why you want to look in my diary, to see if there's anything about you in it."

"Do you go down to the cellar," I said through my laughs, "and sit on that stool and write about us all in your little black book?"

I forced myself to go on laughing. I felt troubled and I needed to make a lot of noise. As I laughed I put my hands on my knees, but I could not quite feel them. Sue watched me as if she was remembering rather than seeing me. She took the book from under her pillow, opened it and looked for a page. I stopped laughing and waited.

"August the ninth. . . . You've been dead nineteen days. No one mentioned you today." She paused, and her eyes ran down several lines. "Jack was in a horrible mood. He hurt Tom on the stairs for making a noise. He made a great scratch across his head and there was quite a lot of blood. At lunch we mixed together two tins of soup. Jack did not talk to anyone. Julie talked about her bloke who is called Derek. She said she might bring him home one time and did we mind. I said no. Jack pretended he didn't hear and went upstairs." Sue found another page and went on reading with more expression. "He has not changed his clothes since you died. He does not wash his hands or anything and he smells horrible. We hate it when he touches a loaf of bread. You can't say anything to him in case he hits you. He's always about to hit someone, but Julie knows how to deal with him. . . ." Sue paused, and seemed about to go on, but changed her mind and snapped the book shut.

"There," she said. For several minutes after we argued wearily about what Julie had said at lunchtime.

"She didn't mention bringing anyone home," I said.

"She did!"

"She didn't." Sue squatted on the floor in front of one of her books and pretended not to notice when I left.

Downstairs the radio was playing louder than I had ever heard it. A man was shouting wildly about a competition. I found Tom sitting at the top of the stairs. He was wearing a blue and white frock which tied up in a bow behind. But his wig was somewhere else. As I sat down beside him I was aware briefly of a faint, unpleasant smell. Tom was crying. He put his knuckles in his eyes the way little girls do on biscuit tin lids. A large tube of green snot hung out of one nostril, and when he sniffed it bobbed out of sight. I watched it for a while. Beyond the sound of the radio I thought I could hear other voices but I was not certain. When I asked Tom why he was crying he cried louder. Then he recovered and whined, "Julie hit me and shouted at me," and he began to cry again.

I left him and went downstairs. The radio was on loud because Julie and Derek were having an argument. I stopped short of the door and tried to listen. Derek seemed to be pleading with Julie; his voice had a whining note. They were both talking, almost shouting, as I came in and they both stopped immediately. Derek leaned against the table, his hands in his pockets and his ankles crossed. He wore a dark green suit and a cravat which was knotted through a gold clasp. Julie stood by the window. I walked between them toward the radio and switched it off. Then I turned and waited for one of them to speak first. I wondered why they did not go out into the garden to shout at each other. Julie said, "What do you want?" She was not dressed up like Derek. She wore plastic sandals and jeans, and had tied her shirt in a knot under her breasts.

"Just came down to see what all the noise was, and who," I said, glancing at Derek, "hit Tom."

Julie tapped her foot slowly to make it clear she was waiting for me to leave.

I walked back between them slowly, putting my heel down just in front of my toes the way people do when they measure a distance without a ruler. Derek cleared his throat very softly and pulled out his watch on the end of its chain. I watched him snap it open, close it and put it away. I had not seen him since the first time he had visited the house over a week ago. But several times now he had called for Julie in his car. I had heard its engine outside and Julie running down the front path but I never looked out the window at them the way Sue and Tom did. Two or three times now Julie had stayed out all night. She never told me where she went but she did tell Sue. The morning after, the two of them would sit in the kitchen for hours, talking and drinking tea. Perhaps Sue wrote it all down in her book without Julie knowing.

Suddenly Derek smiled at me and said, "How are you, Jack?"

Julie sighed noisily. "Don't," she said to him, and

I said very coolly, "All right."

"What are you up to these days?" he said. I looked at Julie as I spoke.

"Nothing much." I could see it irritated her that I was talking to her Derek.

I said, "What about you?"

Derek paused before he spoke and then he sighed, "Practicing. A few small games. Nothing big, you know...."

I nodded.

Derek and Julie were staring at each other. I looked from one to the other and tried to think of something else to say. Without taking his eyes off Julie, Derek said, "Ever played the game yourself?"

If she had not been there I would have said yes. I had watched a game once, and I knew the rules. I said, "Not really."

Derek pulled out his watch again.

"You should come down and have a game."

Julie unfolded her arms and walked quickly out of the room. She gave a little sigh as she went.

Derek watched her go and said, "I mean, are you busy now?"

I thought hard and said, "I'm not all that busy."

Derek stood up and dusted his suit down with his hands which were very small and pale. He went into the hallway to adjust his cravat in the mirror. He called over his shoulder, "You should get a light for out here."

We left by the back and as we were going through the kitchen I noticed that the cellar door was wide open. I hesitated. I wanted to go upstairs and ask Julie about it. But Derek pushed the door shut with his foot and said, "Come on. I'm already late," and we hurried out, up the front garden path toward the low red car.

I was surprised that Derek drove so slowly. He sat upright in his seat and held the wheel at arm's length and between finger and thumb, as if the touch of it disgusted him. He did not speak to me. There were two rows of black dials on the instrument panel, each with a flickering white needle. I watched these for most of the journey. None of the needles really moved its position except those on the clock. We drove for a quarter of an hour. We turned off a main road and went down a narrow street with vegetable warehouses on either side. In some places there were rotting vegetables piled in the gutter. A man in a crumpled suit stood on the pavement staring at us blankly. He had oily hair and a folded newspaper stuck out of his pocket. Derek stopped the car by him and climbed out, leaving the engine running. Behind the man was an alleyway. As we passed him to go down it Derek said to the man, "Park the car and see me inside." At the end of the alley were green swing doors with "Oswald's Hall" scratched into the paint. Derek went in first and held the door open for me with one finger and without turning round. Two games were being played on the tables farthest from us, but nearly all the tables were empty and dark. There was one table in the center of the hall that was all lit up. It seemed brighter than the other two, and the brightly colored balls were set out ready for a game. Someone was leaning against this table with his back to us smoking a cigarette. Cut into the wall behind us was a bright square hole, and through it an old man in a white jacket was looking at us. On a narrow shelf in front of him there were cups and saucers with blue edges and a plastic bowl with one bun inside. Derek stooped down to speak to the man and I walked a few steps away toward one of the tables. I read the name of the maker and his town on a brass plate screwed to the edge right behind the center pocket.

Derek made a clicking sound at me with his tongue. He held a cup of tea in each hand and he jerked his head to make me follow him. With his foot he pushed open a door in the same wall. Next to the door I noticed for the first time a window with one pane of glass missing. A woman with thick glasses sat behind a desk writing in an accounts book and on the other side of the tiny room a man sat in an armchair holding a packet of cigarettes. The smoke made it hard to see. There was just one dim lamp on the edge of the desk. Derek set down the teacups by the lamp and pretended to punch the man on the chin. The man and the woman made a lot of fuss over Derek. They called him "son," but he introduced them to me as "Mr. and Mrs. O for Oswald."

"And this is Julie's brother," Derek said, but he did not tell them my name.

There was nowhere to sit down. Derek took a cigarette from Mr. O's packet. Mrs. O kicked her legs and made a whimpering sound and held up her mouth like a baby bird in a nest. Derek took another cigarette and put it in her mouth and she and Mr. O laughed. Mr O gestured toward the tables.

"Greg's been out there waiting almost an hour, son."

Derek nodded. He was sitting on the edge of the desk, and I was standing by the door. Mrs. O wagged her finger in Derek's face.

"Who's a naughty boy?"

He moved a little farther away from her and reached for his tea. He did not pass me mine.

Mrs. O said carefully, "You didn't come in yesterday then, son."

Mr. O winked at me and said, "He's got other fish to fry."

Derek sipped his tea and said nothing.

Mr. O went on, "But there was quite a crowd in here waiting for you to show up."

Derek nodded and said, "Yeah? Good."

Mrs. O said to me, "He's been coming in here since he was twelve, and we never charge him for a table. Do we son?"

Derek finished his tea and stood up. He said to Mr. O, "Cue, please."

Mr. O stood up and put his slippers on. Along the wall behind him was a rack of cues, and padlocked to one end was a long, tapering leather case. Mr. O wiped his hands on a yellow cloth, unlocked the case and drew the cue out. It was a very dark brown, almost black. Before giving it to Derek he said to me, "I'm the only one he lets touch his cues."

Mrs. O said, "And me," but Mr. O smiled at me and shook his head.

The man who had parked the car was waiting outside the office.

"This is Chas," Derek said, "this is Julie's brother."

Chas and I did not look at each other. As Derek walked slowly toward the center table with his cue, Chas walked on tiptoe beside him, talking quickly into his ear. I walked right behind them. I felt like leaving. Chas was saying something about a horse but Derek did not reply or even turn his head to look at him. As soon as Derek was near the table Greg bent down low to aim his opening shot. He had a brown leather jacket with a big tear in one arm and his hair was tied at the back in a ponytail. I wanted him to win. The white ball drifted the length of the table, dislodged one of the reds and returned to its starting point. Derek took off his jacket and gave it to Chas to hold. He fixed silver bands round his arms to keep his cuffs clear of his wrists. Chas turned the jacket inside out and folded it over his arm and opened his paper to the racing page. Derek ducked down and hit the white ball without appearing to aim. When the dislodged red ball smacked into the bottom pocket, players on the other two tables looked up and walked toward us. Derek's heels made a sharp clicking sound as he strode to the other end of the table. The white had broken up all the reds and was lined up with the black. Before he took his shot Derek glanced up at me to see if I was watching and I looked away.

For the next few minutes he hit reds and the black into the bottom pockets. Between each shot he walked quickly from one side of the table to the other and talked to me in a quiet voice, without looking in my direction, as if he was talking to himself.

"Funny setup in your house," he said as the first black went down. Greg and the other players watched and listened to our conversation.

I said, "I dunno."

"The parents are both dead," Derek said to Chas, "and the four of them looking after themselves."

"Orphans like," Chas said, not looking up from his paper.

"It's a big house," Derek said as he brushed past me to get to the white again.

"Pretty big," I said.

"It must be worth quite a bit." A red disappeared slowly over the lip of a pocket and he was able to aim for a black without changing his position. "All those rooms," he said, "you could turn it into flats."

I said, "We're not thinking of that."

Derek watched Greg pick the black out of the pocket and set it down on its spot.

"And that cellar, not many houses have cellars like that. . . ."

He walked around the table the long way, and Chas sighed at something he was reading. Another red went down. "You could. . . ." Derek was watching to see where the white ball was going to stop. "You could *do* something with that cellar."

"Like what?" I said, but Derek shrugged and hit the black hard into the pocket.

When finally Derek missed a black he made a sharp hissing sound between his teeth.

Chas looked from his paper and said, "Forty-nine."

I said to Derek, "I'm going now," but he had turned away to get a cigarette from one of the other players. Then he walked to the other end of the table to watch Greg.

I felt sick. I leaned back against a pillar and looked up at the ceiling. There were iron girders and beyond them, set in the roof, panes of glass smeared with yellowish brown paint. I looked down and Derek was playing again with only a few balls left on the table. When the game was over Derek came up to me from behind and gripped my elbow and said,

"Want a game?" I told him no and pulled away.

I said, "I'm going back home now."

Derek stood in front of me and laughed. He rested the thick end of his cue against his foot and jigged it up and down.

"You're a queer one," he said. "Why don't you relax a bit, why don't you ever smile?"

I leaned right back against the pillar. Something heavy and dark was pressing down on me and I stared up at the ceiling again, half expecting to see it.

Derek went on jigging his cue, and then he had an idea. He drew in his breath sharply and called over his shoulder, "Hey Chas! Greg! Come and help me make this miserable bugger laugh." He smiled and winked at me as he said this, as if I should be in on the joke too. Chas and Greg appeared on either side of Derek and slightly behind him. "Come on," Derek said, "a big laugh or I'll tell your sister." Their faces grew larger. "Or I'll make Greg tell you one of his jokes." Chas and Greg laughed. Everyone wanted to be on the right side of Derek.

"Fuck off!" I said.

Chas said, "Ah, leave the lad alone," and walked away.

The way he said this made me want to cry and so to show them that this was the last thing I was going to do I stared at Derek fiercely and without blinking. But water was collecting in one eye, and though I snatched at the tear as soon as it rolled out, I knew they had seen it. Greg held out his hand for me to shake.

"No harm meant me old mate," he said. I did not shake it because my hand was wet. Greg walked off, and it was just Derek and me again.

I turned and walked toward the door. Derek left his cue on a table and came with me. We walked so close we could have been handcuffed.

"You're really just like your sister, you are," he said.

Because I could not get by Derek I had to head to the left of the door, toward the tea hatch. As soon as he saw us coming, the old man there took up his big steel teapot and filled two cups. He had a very high-pitched voice.

"You can have these ones on me," he said, "for your forty-nine points." He said it to me as much as to Derek and I had to pick up one of the cups. Derek picked up his too and we leaned against the wall facing each other. For several minutes he seemed about to say something, but he remained silent. I tried to drink the tea quickly and that made me feel hot and sick. Under my shirt my skin prickled and itched, my feet sweated and my toes were slippery against one another. I leaned my head against the wall.

Greg had gone off with Chas through another door, and the other players were back at their tables. Through the wall I heard Mrs. O talking uninterruptedly. After a while I thought it might be the radio.

Derek said, "Is your sister always like this or is there something wrong that I should know about?"

"Always like what?" I said immediately. My heart thudded, but very slowly. Again Derek had to think for a moment. He stretched the skin under his chin and touched his cravat.

"Strictly man to man, you understand?" I nodded. "Take this afternoon for instance. She was doing something, so I thought I'd take a look round your cellar. No harm in that, but she got very funny about it. I mean, there's nothing down there, is there?" I did not think it was a real question and I made no reply. But Derek repeated, "Is there?"

And I said, "No, no. I hardly ever go down there, but there's nothing."

"So why should she get so upset?" Derek stared at me and waited for an answer, as if I were the one who had been upset.

"She's always like that," I told him, "that is what Julie is like."

Derek looked down at his shoes for a moment, looked up and said, "And another time. . . ."

But Mr. O came out of his office just then and started talking to Derek. I finished the rest of my tea and left.

At home the back door was open and I went in very quietly. There were smells in the kitchen of something that had been fried a long time before. I had a strange sensation of having been away several months and that many things had happened in my absence. In the living room Julie was sitting by the table which had dirty plates and a frying pan on it. She was looking very pleased with herself. Tom was sitting on her lap with his thumb in his mouth, and round his neck there was a napkin tied like a bib. He was staring across the room in a glazed kind of way and his head leaned against Julie's breasts. He did not seem to notice that I had come in and went on making small sucking noises with his thumb. Julie rested one hand on the small of his back. She smiled at me and I put my hand on the doorknob to steady myself. I felt as though I weighed nothing and might drift away.

"Don't be so surprised," Julie said, "Tom wants to be a little baby." She rested her chin on his head and began to rock backward and forward slightly. "He was such a naughty boy this afternoon," she went on, talking more to him than to me, "so we had a long talk and decided lots of things." Tom's eyes were closing. I sat down at the table close to Julie but where I could not see Tom's face. I picked at the cold pieces of bacon in the frying pan. Julie rocked and hummed quietly to herself.

Tom was asleep. I had intended to talk to Julie about Derek, but now she stood up with Tom in her arms, and I followed them up the stairs. Julie pushed open the door of the bedroom with her foot. She had brought up from the cellar our old brass cot and put it right by her own bed. It was all made up ready, with one side down. I was annoyed to see the cot and the bed so close together. I pointed and said, "Why didn't you put it in his own room?" Julie had her back to me and was setting Tom down in the cot. He sat swaying slightly as Julie unbuttoned his dress. His eyes were open.

"He wanted it in here, didn't you my sweet?" Tom nodded as he crawled between the sheets. Julie went to the window to draw the curtains. I advanced into the semidarkness and stood at the end of the cot. She pushed by me, kissed Tom's head and carefully raised the side. Tom seemed to be asleep almost instantly. "There's a good boy," Julie whispered, and took my hand and led me out of her bedroom.

# Chapter Nine

NOT LONG after Sue read to me from her diary I
began to notice a smell on my hands. It was sweet
and faintly rotten and was more on the fingers than
the palms, or perhaps even between the fingers. It
was a smell that reminded me of the meat we had
thrown out. I stopped masturbating. I did not feel
like it anyway. After I washed my hands they
smelled only of soap, but if I turned my head away
and moved one hand quickly in front of my nose,
the bad smell was just there, beneath the perfume of
the soap. I took long baths in the middle of the
afternoon and lay perfectly still without a thought
till the water was cold. I cut my nails, washed my
hair and found clean clothes. Within half an hour

the smell was back, so distant that it was more like
the memory of a smell. Julie and Sue made jokes
about my appearance. They said I was dressing up
for a secret girlfriend. However, my new look made
Julie more friendly. She bought me two shirts from
a jumble sale, almost new and a good fit. I
confronted Tom and wiggled my fingers under his
nose. He said, "Like a fishy," in his loud new baby
voice. I found the home medical encyclopedia and
looked up cancer. I thought I might be rotting away
from a slow disease. I looked in the mirror and tried
to catch my breath in my cupped hands. One
evening it rained at last, very heavily. Someone had
once told me that rain was the cleanest water in the
world, so I took my shirt, shoes and socks off and
stood on top of the rockery with my hands stretched
out. Sue came to the kitchen door and, shouting
over the noise of the rain, asked me what I was
doing. She went away and returned with Julie. They
called to me and laughed, and I turned my back on
them.

At supper we had an argument. I said it was the
first time it had rained since Mother died. Julie and
Sue said it had rained several times since. When I
asked them when exactly, they said they could not
remember. Sue said she knew she had used her
umbrella because it was now in her bedroom, and
Julie said she remembered the sound the windshield
wipers made in Derek's car. I said that proved
nothing at all. They became angry which made me
feel calm and intent on making them angrier. Julie
challenged me to prove it had not rained and I said I
did not need to, I *knew* it had not. My sisters gasped
with annoyance. When I asked Sue to pass me the

sugar bowl she ignored me. I walked round the table and just as I was reaching for it she picked up the bowl and put it on the other side of the table, near where I had been sitting. I went to smack her hard on the back of her neck but Julie cried out, "You dare!" so sharply that I drew back startled and my hand swept over the top of Sue's head. Immediately I caught the smell again. As I sat down I waited for Julie or Sue to accuse me of farting, but they began a conversation that was designed to exclude me. I sat on my hands and winked at Tom.

Tom stared at me with his mouth half open and I could see chewed food on his tongue. He sat close to Julie's side. While we were arguing about the rain he had smeared food over his face. Now he was waiting for Julie to remember him, wipe his face with the bib round his neck and tell him he could leave the table. Then he might crawl under the table and sit among our legs while we finished eating.

Other times he tore his bib off and ran outside to play with his friends and would not be a baby again till he came back inside and found Julie. As a baby he rarely spoke or made a noise. He simply waited for her next move. When she babied him his eyes grew larger and farther apart, his mouth slackened and he seemed to sink inside himself.

One evening, as Julie picked Tom up to take him upstairs, I said, "Real babies kick and scream when they get put to bed." Tom glared at me over Julie's shoulder and his eyes and mouth narrowed suddenly.

"No they don't," he said reasonably. "Not always they don't," and let himself be carried out of the room.

I could not resist watching them together. I trailed after them, fascinated, waiting to see what would happen. Julie seemed to enjoy an audience, and she made jokes about it.

"You look so serious," she said once, "like you were watching a funeral." Tom, of course, wanted Julie all to himself.

The second evening I followed them up the stairs again at bedtime and leaned in the doorway while Julie undressed Tom, who had his back to me. Julie smiled at me and asked me to bring Tom's pajamas. Tom turned in the cot and shouted, "Go away! You go away!"

Julie laughed and ruffled his hair and said, "What am I going to do with the two of you?" But I stepped backward out of her room and leaned against the wall in the corridor and listened while Julie read a story. When she came out at last she was not surprised to see me there. We went into my room and sat on the bed. We did not turn the light on. I cleared my throat and said perhaps it was bad for Tom to go on pretending to be a baby.

"Perhaps he won't be able to come out of it," I said.

Julie did not reply at first. I could just make out that she was smiling at me. She put her hand on my knee and said, "I think someone is jealous."

We laughed, and I lay back on the bed. Daringly I touched the small of her back with the ends of my fingers. She shivered and increased the pressure on my knee.

Then Julie had said, "Do you think a lot about Mom?"

I whispered, "Yes, do you?"

"Of course." There seemed nothing more to say, but I wanted us to go on talking.

"Do you think what we did was right?"

Julie took her hand from my knee. She was silent for such a long time I thought she had forgotten my question. I touched her back again and immediately she spoke. "It seemed obvious then, but I don't know now. Perhaps we shouldn't have."

"We can't do anything about it now," I said, and waited for her to disagree. I also waited for her hand to return to my knee. I ran my forefinger the length of her spine and wondered what had changed between us. Had my taking baths made such a difference to her? Finally she said, "No, I suppose not," and folded her arms with a finality that suggested she was offended. One moment she was in charge; the next she was silent, waiting to be attacked.

I said impatiently, "You let Derek into the cellar."

Now everything was changed between us. Julie crossed the room, turned on the light and stood by the door. She tossed her head irritably to clear a strand of hair from her face. I sat right on the edge of the bed and put my hand on my knee where hers had been.

"Is that what he told you when you were playing...billiards?"

"I only watched."

"He found the key and went down there to look around," Julie said.

"You should have stopped him." She shook her head. It was unusual for her to plead and her voice was unfamiliar.

"He just took the key. There is nothing to see down there."

I said, "You got really angry about it and now he wants to know why."

For once I was getting the better of Julie in an argument. I started to beat out a rhythm with my hands on my knees and briefly caught the sweet, rotten smell.

Suddenly Julie said, "You know, I haven't slept with him or anything like that."

I went on drumming and did not look up. Then, exultant, I stopped and said, "So what?" But Julie had left the room.


LEANING ACROSS the table I caught hold of Tom's bib and pulled him toward me. He gave out a little whimper and then a scream. Julie broke off her conversation and tried to prize my fingers loose. Sue stood up.

"What are you doing?" Julie shouted. "Let go of him." I had pulled Tom a good way along the table when I let go and he fell back into Julie's arms.

"I was going to wipe his mouth for him," I said, "seeing you were so busy talking." Tom hid his face in Julie's lap and began to cry, a good imitation of a baby's wail.

"Why can't you leave people alone?" Sue cried. "What's wrong with you?"

I wandered out into the garden. The rain was stopping. The tower blocks were ugly with fresh stains, but the weeds on the land beyond our garden already looked greener. I walked around the garden the way Father had always wanted everyone to go, along the tiny paths, down the steps to the pond. It was hard to find the steps under the weeds and thistles and the pond was a curling piece of dirty blue plastic. A little rainwater had collected in the bottom. As I walked round the pond I felt something soft collapse under my foot. I had trodden on a frog. It lay on its side with one long back leg stuck in the air, quivering in little circles. A creamy green substance was spilling out of its stomach and the sac under its chin blew in and out very rapidly. With one bulging eye it stared up at me in a sorrowful, unaccusing kind of way. I knelt down beside it and picked up a large flat stone. Now it seemed to look at me expecting help. I waited, hoping it would recover or die suddenly. But the air sac was filling and emptying faster, and it was attempting hopelessly to use its other back leg to right itself. Its small front legs made swimming movements in the air. The yellowish eye stared into mine.

"That's enough," I said out loud and brought the flat stone down sharply on the small green head. When I lifted the stone the frog's body stuck to it and then dropped to the ground. I began to cry. I found another stone and dug a short deep trench. As I pushed it in with a stick I saw its front legs tremble. I covered it quickly with earth and stamped the grave flat.

I heard footsteps behind me and Derek's voice.

"What's wrong with you?" He stood with his legs well apart and slung over his shoulder was a white raincoat which he held hooked with one finger.

"Nothing," I said. Derek came closer.

"What have you got in the ground?"

"Nothing." With the wedge-shaped tip of his polished boot Derek prodded the earth.

"It's a dead frog I just buried," I said.

But Derek kept on digging till he turned over the frog's body, all caked in dirt.

"Look," he said, "it's not dead at all." He sunk and twisted his heel into my frog and covered it with earth again. He did all this with one foot and without taking the raincoat from his shoulder. He smelled of perfume, some kind of after-shave or cologne. I walked farther up the garden toward the little path that wound round the rockery. Derek followed right behind me, and we spiraled up, passing each other in tight little circles like children in a game.

"Julie's in, is she?" he said.

I told him she was putting Tom to bed, and then, when we were balancing very close to each other at the top, I said, "He sleeps in her bedroom now."

Derek nodded quickly as if he already knew and squeezed his tie knot.

We stared at our house. We were so close that when he spoke I smelled peppermint on his breath.

"He's an odd one, your little brother, isn't he? I mean, putting on girls' dresses. . . ." He smiled at me and seemed to expect me to smile too.

But I folded my arms and said, "What's odd about that?"

Derek climbed off the rockery, using the paths as steps, and when he got to the bottom he spent some time folding his raincoat over his arm. He coughed and said, "It could affect him in later life, you know."

I climbed off the rockery too, and we walked toward the house.

"What do you mean by that?" I asked him. We were standing outside the kitchen door. Derek stared through the window and did not reply. The door to the living room was open and we could see Sue sitting alone reading a magazine.

Suddenly Derek said, "When did your parents die exactly?"

"Long time ago," I muttered and pushed open the kitchen door. Derek caught hold of my arm.

"Wait," he said. "Julie told me it was recently." Sue called out my name from the living room. I pulled my arm free and went indoors. Derek whispered after me to come back and then I heard him wiping his feet carefully before stepping into the kitchen.

As soon as Derek came into the room Sue dropped her magazine and ran into the kitchen to make him a cup of tea. She treated him like a film star. He walked about with his coat folded in a neat square looking for a place to put it down and Sue watched him from the doorway like a frightened rabbit. I sat down and looked at Sue's magazine. Derek set his coat down on the floor by a chair and sat down too. Sue said from the kitchen, "Julie's upstairs with Tom." Her voice was all shaky.

"I'll wait down here then," Derek called out. He crossed his legs and plucked at his shirt cuffs so they protruded the right distance from under his suit. I turned the pages of the magazine without taking anything in. When Derek took the cup of tea from Sue he said, "Thank you, Susan," in a funny voice and she giggled and sat down as far away from him as possible. It was while he was stirring his tea that he looked straight across at me and said, "There's a funny smell in here. Have you noticed it?"

I shook my head but I could feel myself blushing. Derek watched me and sipped. He lifted his head and sniffed loudly.

"It's not a strong smell," he said, "but it's very odd."

Sue stood up and began to talk rapidly.

"It's the drain outside the kitchen. It gets blocked very easily and in the summer... you know...." Then, after a pause, she said again, "It's the drain."

Derek nodded while she was talking and looked at me. Sue went back to her chair and for a long time after that no one spoke.

None of us heard Julie come in the room, and when she spoke Derek gave a start.

"All very quiet," she said softly.

Derek stood up straight like a soldier and said very politely, "Good evening, Julie."

Sue giggled. Julie was wearing her velvet skirt and had tied her hair back with a white ribbon.

Derek said, "We were talking about the drains," and with a stiff little movement of his hand tried to direct Julie into his chair. But she came and settled herself on the arm of mine.

"Drains?" she said as if to herself, but did not seem to want to know more.

"And how have you been?" Derek said.

Sue giggled again and we all turned to look at her. Julie pointed at Derek's coat.

"Why don't you hang it up before someone treads on it?"

Derek lifted his coat onto his lap and stroked it.

"Nice pussy," he said, and no one laughed. Sue asked Julie if Tom was asleep.

"Out like a light," Julie said. Derek took out his

watch and looked at it. We all knew what he was
going to say.

"A bit early isn't it? For Tom?"

This time Sue had a fit of giggling. She clasped
her hands over her face and hobbled into the
kitchen. We heard her open the door and go outside
into the garden. Julie was very cool.

"In fact," she said, "it's a bit later than usual, isn't
it Jack?" I nodded, although I had no idea what time
it was.

Julie ruffled my hair.

"Haven't you noticed a difference in him?" she
said to Derek.

"Cleaner and smarter," he said instantly. He said
to me, "Pulling the ladies now are you?"

Julie rested her hand on my head.

"Oh no," she said, "we're having none of that
round here."

Derek laughed and took out his cigarettes. When
he offered one to Julie she refused. I kept very still
because I did not want her to move her hand. At the
same time I sensed I looked foolish to Derek. He
settled back in his chair and smoked his cigarette,
watching us all the time. We heard Sue open the
back door, but she remained in the kitchen.
Suddenly Derek smiled and I wondered whether,
behind me, Julie was smiling too. They stood up at
the same time without speaking. Before she took her
hand off my head, Julie gave it a little pat.

As soon as they were upstairs Sue returned and
sat on the edge of Derek's chair. She laughed
nervously and said, "I know what that smell is."

"It isn't me."

She led me into the kitchen and unlocked the

cellar door. It was, of course, the same smell, I knew that at once, but it was changed by being intensified. Now it was separate from me. There was something sweet, and beyond that, or wrapped around it, another bigger, softer smell that was like a fat finger pushing into the back of my throat. It rolled up the concrete steps out of the darkness. I breathed through my mouth.

"Go on," Sue said, "go down. You know what it is," and she turned on the light and pushed me in the small of my back.

"Only if you come too," I said.

There was a rustling sound from somewhere along the corridor that led from the bottom of the stairs to the end room. Sue stepped back into the kitchen and picked up a plastic toy torch belonging to Tom. It was in the shape of a fish. Its light came from its mouth and was very weak.

I said, "There's plenty of light. We don't need that."

But she was prodding me in the back with it.

"Go on, you'll see," she whispered.

At the foot of the stairs we stopped to turn on another set of lights. Sue put a handkerchief over her nose, and I covered my face with my shirttails. The door at the end of the corridor was half open. From in there we heard the rustling sound again.

"Rats," Sue said. When we reached the door the room was suddenly silent and I stopped.

"Push," Sue said through her handkerchief.

I did not move, but now the door was opening on its own. I cried out and stepped backward and saw that my sister was pressing with her foot near the hinge. The trunk looked as if it had been kicked. The middle bulged right out. The surface of the concrete was broken by a huge crack in some places half an inch wide. Sue wanted me to look down it. She put the torch in my hand, pointed and said something I could not hear. As I shone the light along the crack I remembered a time when Commander Hunt and his crew flew low across the surface of an unknown planet. Thousands of miles of flat, hard-baked desert broken only by great fissures caused by earthquakes. Not one hill or tree or house and no water. There was no wind because there was no air. They flew away into space without landing, and no one spoke for hours.

Sue uncovered her mouth and whispered fiercely, "What are you waiting for?"

I leaned over the crack at its widest point and shone the torch down. I saw a convoluted yellowish gray surface. Round the edge was something black and frayed. As I stared, the surface formed itself briefly into a face, an eye, part of a nose and a dark mouth. The image dissolved into convoluted surfaces once more. I thought I was about to fall over and gave the torch to Sue. But the feeling passed as I watched her bending over the trunk. We went into the corridor and closed the door behind us.

"Did you see?" Sue said. "The sheet is all torn and you can see her nightie underneath." For a moment we were very excited, as if we had discovered that our mother was in fact alive. We had seen her in her nightie, just the way she was.

As we were going up the stairs I said, "The smell isn't too bad once you get used to it."

Sue half laughed and half sobbed and dropped

the torch. Behind us we could hear the rats again. She took deep breaths and bent down to pick up the torch. As she stood up she said, "We'll have to get more cement," and her voice was quite level.

At the top of the stairs we met Derek. Over his shoulder I could see Julie in the center of the kitchen. Derek blocked our way out of the cellar.

"Well, you're not very good at keeping secrets," he said in a friendly way. "What have you got down there that smells so good?"

We pushed by him without replying. Sue stood at the sink and drank water from a teacup. The sound of the liquid going down her throat was very loud.

I said, "It's none of your business really."

I turned to Julie, hoping she would think of something to say. She walked to where Derek stood in the cellar doorway and tried to pull him gently by the arm.

"Let's lock the door," she said, "that smell is getting on my nerves."

But Derek pulled his arm away and once again said in a friendly way, "But you haven't told me what it is yet."

He brushed the arm of his jacket where Julie had pulled and smiled at us. "I'm very curious you see." We watched him turn and descend the stairs. We heard his footsteps stop at the bottom as he fumbled for the light switch, and continue to the room at the end. And then we followed him down, first Julie, then Sue, then me.

Derek took a pale blue handkerchief from his breast pocket, shook it out and held it not over his face but near it. I was determined to use nothing and took quick breaths between my teeth. Derek tapped the trunk with his boot. My sisters and I stood in a shallow circle behind him, as if some important ceremony were about to take place. He traced with his finger the line of the crack and peered into it.

"Whatever's in there is really rotten."

"It's a dead dog," Julie said suddenly and simply, "Jack's dog."

Derek grinned.

I said, "You promised you wouldn't say."

Julie shrugged and said, "It doesn't matter now."

Derek was bending over the trunk. Julie went on, "It's his idea of a...a tomb. He put her in there when she died and poured concrete all over her." Derek broke off a piece of concrete and tossed it in his hand.

"You didn't make a very good job of the mix," he said, "and this trunk isn't holding the weight."

"The smell is all over the house," Julie said to me, "you'd better do something about it." Derek wiped his hands carefully on his handkerchief.

"I think it calls for a reburial," he said, "in the garden, perhaps. Next to your frog." I went over to the trunk and kicked it gently the way Derek had done.

"I don't want it moved," I said firmly. "Not after all that work."

Derek led the way out of the cellar. When we were upstairs we all went into the living room. Derek asked me the name of my dog, and without thinking I said, "Cosmo."

He came and put his hand on my shoulder and said, "We'll have to seal that crack with cement then and hope the trunk will hold."

For the rest of the evening we sat about, doing

nothing. Derek talked about snooker. Much later, as I was going to my bedroom, he said, "I'll show you how to make a proper mix this time," and from the stairs I heard Julie say, "It's best to leave him to it. He doesn't like you showing him what to do."

Derek said something I could not hear and then laughed to himself for rather a long time.

# Chapter Ten

THE HOT weather returned. In the morning Julie sunbathed on the rockery, this time without her radio. Tom, who was wearing his own clothes for the first time in days, played in the garden with his friend from the tower block. Whenever Tom was about to do something he considered particularly daring, like jumping over a stone, he wanted Julie to watch him.

"Julie, watch! Julie! Julie, look!" I heard his voice all morning. I went to watch them from the kitchen. Julie lay on a bright blue towel and ignored Tom. Her skin was so dark I thought it would only be another day before it was black. There were several wasps in the kitchen feeding off rubbish that had spilled across the floor. Outside there was a cloud of flies round the overflowing dustbins which had not been emptied for weeks. We thought there might have been a strike but we had heard nothing. A packet of butter had melted into a pool. While I watched out the window, I dabbed my finger in it and sucked. Today it was too hot to clean the kitchen. Sue came and told me that already it was a record; she had heard on the radio that it was the hottest day since 1900.

"Julie should be careful," Sue said, and went outside to warn her. But neither Tom and his friend nor Julie seemed touched by the heat. She lay quite still, and they chased each other round the garden shouting each other's name.

In the late afternoon I walked to the shops with Julie to buy a packet of cement. Tom came too. He kept close by Julie's side and held onto a corner of her white skirt. At one point I had to stand in the shade of a bus shelter to recover from the heat. Julie stood in front of me in the sunlight trying to fan me with her hand.

"What's the matter with you?" she said. "You look so weak. What have you been doing with yourself?" She caught my eye and we both laughed. Outside the shop we saw our reflections in the plate glass window. Julie locked her hand into mine and said, "Look how pale yours are." I pulled my hand away and as we were going into the shop she spoke to me firmly as if I was a child.

"You really ought to get out in the sun. It will do you good." On the way home I thought of a time not long ago when Julie had never spoken unless spoken to. Now she was talking excitedly to Tom about circuses, and once she stopped and knelt by him and with a paper tissue wiped his lips clean of ice cream and snot.

When we arrived at our front gate I decided that I did not want to return indoors. Julie took the ten-pound bag of cement from me and said, "That's right, you stay out in the sun."

As I walked up our street I noticed suddenly how different it looked. It was hardly a street at all; it was a road across an almost empty junkyard. There were only two other houses left standing apart from ours. Ahead of me a group of workmen stood round a builders' lorry preparing to go home. The lorry was starting up just as I reached it. Three men were standing on the back holding onto the rack on top of the driver's cab. One of the men saw me and jerked his head sideways in greeting. Then, as the lorry bounced over the curb he pointed in the direction of our house and shrugged. All that was left of the prefabs were the big slabs of the foundations. I went and stood on one. Running across the slab were grooves where the walls had been. Weeds that looked like small lettuces grew in the grooves. I walked along the lines of the walls, placing one foot just in front of the other, and thought how strange it was that a whole family could live inside this rectangle of concrete. It was hard to tell now if this was the prefab I had visited before. There was nothing to tell them apart. I took off my shirt and spread it on the floor in the center of the largest room. I lay down on my back and stretched out my hands on the ground so that my fingers caught the sun. Immediately I felt stifled by the heat, my skin prickled with sweat. But determined, I stayed where I was and daydreamed.

When I woke up I wondered why I was not in my bed. I shivered and felt for my sheets. When I stood up my head began to ache. I picked up my shirt and walked home slowly, stopping once to admire the blood red color of my chest and arms, deepened by the evening sunlight. Derek's car was parked outside the house. As I entered the kitchen I saw the cellar door open and heard voices and scraping noises.

Derek had rolled his sleeves up and was forcing wet cement down the crack with a trowel. Julie stood watching him with her hands on her hips.

"Doing your chores for you," Derek said as I came in, but he was obviously enjoying himself. Julie seemed delighted to see me, as if I had been away at sea for years.

"Look at you," she said, "you've really caught it. You look lovely. Doesn't he look lovely?"

Derek grunted and leaned over his work. Already the smell was less noticeable. Derek whistled softly through his teeth as he smoothed down the cement. While his back was to us Julie winked at me and I pretended I was about to kick Derek in the backside.

Sensing something, Derek said without turning round, "Anything wrong?"

"No, nothing," we said together, and we began to laugh.

Derek came toward me with the trowel. To my surprise he sounded hurt.

"Perhaps you better do it," he said.

"Oh no," I said, "you're much better at it than I am."

Derek was trying to put the trowel into my hands.

"It's your dog," he said, "if it *is* a dog."

"Derek!" Julie said soothingly. "Please do it. You said you would." She led him back to the trunk. "If Jack does it, it will only crack again and the smell will be everywhere." Derek shrugged and began his work again. Julie patted him on the shoulder and picked up his jacket which was hanging on a nail. She folded it over her arm and patted that too. "Nice pussy," she whispered.

This time Derek ignored our soft giggles.

He finished the job and stood back. Julie said, "Well done!" Derek made her a little bow and tried to hold her hand. I said something similar, but he did not look in my direction. Upstairs in the kitchen Julie and I stood in attendance while Derek washed his hands. Julie offered him a towel, and as he was drying his hands, he tried to draw her toward him. But Julie came and put her hand on my shoulder and admired the color in my face.

"You look so much better," she said, "doesn't he?"

Derek was knotting his tie with quick, sharp movements. Julie appeared to have complete control of his moods. He adjusted his cuffs and reached for his jacket.

"Looks to me like he overdid it," he said.

He moved toward the door, and for a moment I thought he was going to leave. Instead he stooped down and picked up an old teabag by its corner and threw it in the direction of the wastebin. Julie filled the kettle and I wandered into the living room to look for teacups.

When it was finally ready, we drank the tea standing up in the kitchen. Now he was back in his suit and with his tie on, Derek was more like his old self. He stood very erect, holding his cup in one hand and saucer in the other.

He asked me questions about school and jobs. Then he said carefully, "You must have been very attached to that dog."

I nodded and waited for Julie to change the subject.

"When did he die?" Derek asked.

I said, "It was a she."

There was a pause, and then Derek said a little sulkily, "Well, when did she die?"

"About two months ago." Derek turned to Julie and looked at her pleadingly. She smiled and filled his cup. He spoke into the space between her and me.

"What kind of dog?"

"Oh, you know," Julie said, "a mixture of things."

I added, "But mostly Labrador," and briefly, from somewhere, a dog seemed to lift its sunken eyes to mine. I shook my head.

"Do you mind talking about it?" Derek asked.

"No."

"What gave you the idea of putting her down there?"

"Sort of like preserving her. Like the Egyptians."

Derek nodded curtly as if everything was explained.

Just then Tom came in, ran to Julie and clung to

her leg. We shifted our positions to make the circle a little wider. Derek tried to touch Tom's head, but Tom pushed his hand away and some of Derek's tea spilled on the floor.

He stared at the splashes a moment and said, "Did you like Cosmo, Tom?"

Still holding onto Julie's leg, Tom leaned backward to look at Derek and laughed as if this was a running joke between them.

"You remember Cosmo, our dog," Julie told him rapidly.

Tom nodded. Derek said, "Yes, Cosmo. Were you sad when she died?"

Again Tom swung back and this time stared up at his sister.

"You sat on my lap and cried, don't you remember?"

"Yes," he said mischievously. We all watched Tom closely. "I cried, didn't I?" he said to Julie.

"That's right, and I carried you to bed, remember?"

Tom leaned his head against Julie's belly and seemed deep in reflection. Anxious to get Tom away from Derek, Julie set down her cup and led Tom into the garden. As they were going through the door, Tom said loudly, "A dog!" and laughed derisively.

Derek rattled his car keys in his pocket. Julie was racing Tom across the garden and we both watched through the window. She looked so beautiful as she turned to encourage Tom that it irritated me to share the sight of her with Derek. Without turning from the window he said wistfully, "I wish you would all ... well, trust me a little more."

I yawned. Sue, Julie and I had not talked about our dog story together. We had not been at all careful with Derek. Often what was in the cellar did not seem real enough to keep secret. When we were not actually down there looking at the trunk it was as if we were asleep. Derek took out his watch. "I've got a game. See you later tonight perhaps."

He stepped outside and called to Julie who paused only briefly in her game with Tom to wave to him and blow him a kiss. He waited a moment before walking away, but her back was already turned.

I went to my bedroom, took off my shoes and socks and lay down on the bed. Through my window I could see a clear square of pale blue sky, not one cloud. After less than a minute I sat up and stared about me. On the floor were Coca-Cola tins, dirty clothes, fish and chip wrappers, several wire coat hangers, a box that once contained rubber bands. I stood up and looked at where I had been lying, the folds and rucks in the yellowish gray sheets, large stains with distinct edges. I felt stifled. Everything I looked at reminded me of myself. I opened wide the doors of my wardrobe and threw in all the debris from the floor. I pulled the sheets, blankets and pillows off my bed and put those in too. I ripped down pictures from the wall that I had once cut out of magazines. Under the bed I found plates and cups covered in green mold. I took every loose object and put it in the wardrobe till the room was bare. I even took down the light bulb and light shade. Then I took my clothes off, threw them in and closed the doors. The room was empty like a cell. I lay down on the bed again and stared at my patch of clear sky till I fell asleep.

It was dark and cold when I woke up, With my eyes closed I felt for the bedclothes. I had a confused memory of lying in the prefab. Was I still there? I had no idea how I came to be lying naked on a bare mattress. Someone was crying. Was it me? I knelt up to close the window and remembered suddenly that my mother had died a long time ago. At once everything fell into place and I lay down shivering and listened. The crying was soft and continuous like a moan and it came from the next room. It was soothing, and for a while I listened only to the sound. I had no curiosity beyond that. I stopped shivering and closed my eyes and immediately, as if a show had been delayed till I had settled down, I saw a set of vivid pictures. I opened my eyes briefly and saw the same images imposed on the darkness. I wondered why it was I needed to sleep so much. I saw a crowded beach on a very hot afternoon. It was time to go home. My mother and father were walking ahead of me carrying deck chairs and a bundle of towels. I could not keep up. The large, round pebbles hurt my feet. In my hand there was a stick with a windmill on the end. I was crying because I was tired and I wanted to be carried. My parents stopped to wait for me, but when I was within a few feet of them, they turned and went on. My crying became a long wail and other children stopped what they were doing to look at me. I let go of the windmill and when someone picked it up and offered it to me I shook my head and wailed louder. My mother gave her deck chair to my father and walked toward me. When she picked me up I found myself looking backward over her shoulder at a girl who held my windmill and stared at me. The breeze turned the bright sails and I desperately wanted it back, but already she was a long way beyond us and now we were on the pavement and my mother's stride was rhythmic. I kept on crying to myself but my mother did not seem to hear.

This time I opened my eyes and woke completely. With the windows closed my small room was hot and airless. Next door Tom was still crying. I stood up and fell dizzily against the wardrobe. I opened it and felt for my clothes. The light bulb rolled out and broke on the floor. I swore in a loud whisper. I felt too stifled by both the darkness and lack of air to go on searching. I walked toward the door with my hands stretched out in front of me and my face screwed up. I stood on the landing, waiting for my eyes to adjust to the light. Downstairs Julie and Sue were talking. At the sound of my door opening Tom had gone silent, but now he started again, a forced, unconvincing kind of crying which Julie would take no notice of. Her bedroom door was open, and I went in quietly. The room was lit by a very weak bulb, and Tom did not notice me at first. He had kicked the blankets and sheets to the bottom of the cot and he lay on his back naked, looking up at the ceiling. The sound he was making was like a dull kind of singing. Sometimes he seemed to forget he was crying altogether and fell silent; then he remembered and began again louder. For five minutes or so I stood behind him listening. One arm was flung right behind his head and with the other hand he played with his penis, pulling it and rolling it between his forefinger and thumb.

"Wotcha," I said. Tom tilted his head back and looked at me without surprise. Then his gaze returned to the ceiling and he resumed his crying. I leaned over the side of the cot and said roughly, "What's wrong with you? Why don't you shut up?" Tom's crying became the real, clucking kind, tears spilled onto the sheet by his head. "Wait," I said and tried to lower the cot side. In the gloom I could not see how to release the catch. My brother drew a huge lungful of air and screamed. It was difficult to concentrate; I banged at the catch with my fist; I took hold of the vertical bars and shook them till the whole cot rocked. Tom started to laugh, something gave and the side dropped away.

In his baby voice he called, "Again! I want you to do that again." I sat down at one end of the cot on the pile of sheets and blankets. We stared at each other, and presently he said in his ordinary voice, "Why haven't you got any clothes on?"

I said, "Because I'm hot." He nodded.

"I'm hot too." He lay back with his arms folded behind his head, more like a sunbather now than an infant.

"Was that why you were crying? Because you were hot?"

He thought for a moment before nodding.

I said, "Crying makes you hotter."

"I wanted Julie to come up. She said she would come up and see me."

"Why did you want her to come up?"

"Because I wanted her to."

"But why?" Tom clicked his tongue in exasperation.

"Because I *wanted* her."

I folded my arms. I felt in the mood for an interrogation.

"Do you remember Mum?" He opened his

mouth a little way and nodded. "Don't you want her?"

"She's dead," Tom said indignantly. I settled down in the cot. Tom moved over to make room for my legs.

I said, "Even though she's dead, don't you wish she would come up and see you instead of Julie?"

"I've been in her room," Tom boasted. "I know where Julie keeps the key."

Her locked bedroom hardly ever entered my mind. When I thought of Mother I thought of the cellar. I said, "What do you do in there?"

"Nothing."

"What's in there?" There was a slight whine in Tom's voice.

"Julie put everything away. All Mum's things."

"What did you want with Mum's things?" Tom stared at me as if my question had no meaning. "You played with her things?" I asked.

Tom nodded and pursed his lips in imitation of Julie.

"We did dressing up and things."

"You and Julie?" Tom giggled.

"Me and Michael, stupid!" Michael was Tom's friend from the towers blocks.

"You dressed up in Mum's clothes?"

"Sometimes we were Mummy and Daddy and sometimes we were Julie and you and sometimes we were Julie and Derek."

"What did you do when you were me and Julie?" Again my question meant nothing to Tom. "I mean, what did you *do?*"

"Just play," Tom said vaguely.

Because of the way the light was on his face, and because he had secrets, Tom seemed like a tiny, wise old man lying at my feet. I wondered if he believed in heaven. I said, "Do you know where Mum is now?"

Tom stared up at the ceiling and said, "In the cellar."

"What do you mean?" I whispered.

"In the cellar. In that trunk under all that stuff."

"Who told you that?"

"Derek said. He said you put her in there." Tom turned on his side and put his thumb not in but near his mouth. I shook his ankle.

"When did he tell you that?" Tom shook his head. He never knew whether something happened yesterday or last week. "What else did Derek say?"

Tom sat up and grinned. "He said you keep pretending it's a dog." He laughed. "A dog!"

Tom covered himself with one corner of the sheet and rolled on his side again. He put the tip of his thumb between his lips, but his eyes remained open. I arranged a pillow behind my back. I liked it here in Tom's bed. Everything I had just heard did not matter to me. I felt like raising the cot's side and sitting all night. The last time I had slept here everything had been watched over and arranged. When I was four I had believed it was my mother who devised the dreams I had at night. If she asked me in the morning, as she sometimes did, what I had dreamed, it was to hear if I could tell the truth. I gave up the cot to Sue long before that, when I was two, but lying in it now it was familiar to me—its salty, clammy smell, the arrangement of the bars, an enveloping pleasure in being tenderly imprisoned. A long time passed. Tom's eyes opened briefly and closed again. He sucked his thumb deeper into his mouth. I did not want him to fall asleep yet.

"Tom," I whispered, "Tom. Why do you want to be a baby?"

He spoke in a thin whine as if he were about to weep.

"You're *squashing* me, you are." He kicked at me feebly from under the sheet. "You're squashing me, and it's my bed . . . you. . . ." His voice failed and his eyes closed firmly as his breathing settled into a deep rhythm. I watched him for a minute or so till a faint sound made me aware that I too was being watched from the doorway.

"Look at this," Julie whispered to herself as she crossed the room. "Just look at *you*." She punched me on the shoulder and put her hand over her mouth to stifle her laughter.

"Two bare babies!" She lifted and secured the side and, leaning her elbows over the cot, smiled at me in delight. She had put her hair up and long fine strands of it curled down by her ears from which hung earrings of brightly colored glass beads. "You sweet little thing."

She stroked my head. Her white cotton blouse was unbuttoned down to the swell of her breasts and her skin was a deep, dull brown. She pursed her lips but her smile kept pulling them apart. The sweet, sharp smell of her perfume wrapped itself around me and I sat there grinning foolishly, staring into her eyes. For a joke I thought of putting my thumb in my mouth and lifted my hand to my face.

"Go on," she encouraged, "don't be afraid." The flat taste of my own skin brought me back to myself.

"I'm getting out," I said, and as I knelt up, Julie pointed through the bars.

"Look! It's big!" and she laughed and made as if to grab me.

I climbed over the side, and while Julie covered Tom with a blanket, I edged toward the door, already regretting that I had brought our scene to an end. Julie caught me by the arm and steered me toward the bed.

"Don't go away yet," she said. "I want to talk to you."

We sat facing each other. Julie's eyes were wild and bright-looking. "You look lovely without your clothes," she said. "Pink and white like an ice cream." She touched my sunburned arm. "Is it sore?"

I shook my head and said, "What about your clothes?"

She undressed briskly. When her clothes were between us in a small pile on the bed, she nodded toward Tom and said, "What do you think of him? Don't you think he's happy?"

I said "yes" and told her what he had told me. Julie opened her mouth wide in pretend surprise.

"Derek's known for ages. We haven't been very good at keeping it a secret. What upsets him is that we don't let him in on it." She tittered into her hand. "He feels left out when we go on telling him it's a dog." She moved a little closer to me and wrapped her arms about her body. "He wants to be one of the family, you know, big smart daddy. He's getting on my nerves."

I touched her on the arm the way she had touched me. "Since he knows," I said, "we might as well tell him. I feel a bit daft going on about that dog." Julie shook her head and locked her fingers into mine.

"He wants to take charge of everything. He keeps talking about moving in with us." She squared her shoulders and puffed out her chest. "What you four need is taking care of." I took Julie's other hand and we moved so that we sat with our knees touching. From the cot, which was right up against the bed, Tom murmured in his sleep and swallowed loudly. Julie was whispering now. "He lives with his mum in this tiny house. I've been there. She calls him Doodle and makes him wash his hands before tea." Julie pulled her hands free and placed them on each side of my face. She glanced down between my legs. "She told me she irons fifteen shirts a week for him."

"That's a lot," I said. Julie was squashing my face so that my lips pushed out like a bird's beak.

"You used to look like this all the time," she said, "and now you look like this." She relaxed her hold.

I wanted us to keep talking. I said, "You haven't done any running for a long time."

Julie stretched a leg and laid it across my knee. We both looked at it as if it were a pet. I held the foot in both hands.

"Perhaps I'll do some in the winter," Julie said.

"Are you going back to school next week?" She shook her head.

"Are you?"

"No."

We hugged each other and our arms and legs were in such a tangle that we fell sideways onto the bed. We lay with our arms round each other's necks and our faces close together. For a long time we talked about ourselves.

"It's funny," Julie said, "I've lost all sense of time. It feels like it's always been like this. I can't really remember how it used to be when Mum was alive and I can't really imagine anything changing. Everything seems still and fixed and it makes me feel that I'm not frightened of anything."

I said, "Except for the times I go down into the cellar I feel like I'm asleep. Whole weeks go by without me noticing, and if you asked me what happened three days ago I wouldn't be able to tell you."

We talked about the demolition at the end of our street and what it would be like if they knocked down our house.

"Someone would come poking around," I said, "and all they would find would be a few broken bricks in the long grass." Julie closed her eyes and crossed her leg over my thigh. Part of my arm was against her breast and beneath it I could feel the thud of her heart.

"It wouldn't matter," she murmured, "would it?" She began to edge farther up the bed till her large pale breasts were level with my face. I touched a nipple with the end of my finger. It was hard and wrinkled like a peach stone. Julie took it between her fingers and kneaded it. Then she pushed it toward my lips.

"Go on," she whispered. I felt weightless, tumbling through space with no sense of up or down. As I closed my lips around Julie's nipple a soft shudder ran through her body and a voice from across the room said mournfully, "Now I've seen it all."

Immediately I tried to pull away. But Julie still

had her arms around my neck and she tightened her hold. Her body screened me from Derek. Supporting herself on one elbow, she twisted round to look at him.

"Have you?" she said mildly. "Oh dear." But her heart, inches from my face, was pounding. Derek spoke again and sounded much closer.

"How long has this been going on?" I was glad I could not see him.

"Ages," Julie said, "ages and ages."

Derek made a little gasping sound of surprise or anger. I imagined him standing still and upright with his hands in his pockets. This time his voice was thick and uneven.

"All those times...you never even let me come near you." He cleared his throat noisily and there was a short silence. "Why didn't you tell me?" I felt Julie shrug. Then she said, "Actually, it's none of your business."

"If you'd have told me," Derek said, "I would have cleared off, left you to it."

"Typical!" Julie said. "That's typical." Now Derek was angry. His voice retreated across the room.

"It's sick," he said loudly, "he's your *brother*."

"Talk quietly, Derek," Julie said firmly, "or you'll wake Tom up."

"Sick!" Derek repeated, and the bedroom door slammed shut.

Julie sprang off the bed, locked the door and leaned against it. We listened for Derek's car starting but apart from Tom's breathing everything was very quiet. Julie was smiling at me. She went to the window and parted the curtains a little way.

Derek had been in the room such a short time that now it seemed as though we had imagined him.

"Probably downstairs," Julie said as she settled herself beside me again, "probably moaning at Sue."

We were quiet for a minute or two, waiting for the echoes of Derek's voice to die away. Then Julie laid her palm on my belly. "Look how white you are," she said, "against my hand."

I took her hand and measured it against mine. It was exactly the same size. We sat up and compared the lines on our palms, and these were entirely different. We began a long investigation of each other's bodies. Lying on our backs side by side we compared our feet. Her toes were longer than mine and more slender. We measured our arms, legs, necks and tongues, but none of these looked so alike as our belly buttons, the same fine slit in the whorl which was squashed to one side, the same pattern of creases in the hollow. It went on until I had my fingers in Julie's mouth counting her teeth and we began to laugh at what we were doing.

I rolled onto my back and Julie, still laughing, sat astride me, took hold of my penis and pulled it into her. It was done very quickly and we were suddenly quiet and unable to look at each other. Julie held her breath. There was something soft in my way and as I grew larger inside her it parted and I was deep inside. She gave out a little sigh and knelt forward and kissed me lightly on the lips. She lifted herself slightly and sank down. A cool thrill unfurled from my belly and I sighed too. Finally we looked at each other. Julie smiled and said, "It's easy." I sat up a little way and pressed my face into her breasts. She

took a nipple between her fingers again and found
my mouth. As I sucked and that same shudder ran
through my sister's body, I heard and felt a deep,
regular pulse, a great, dull, slow thudding which
seemed to rise through the house and shake it. I fell
back and Julie crouched forward. We moved slowly
in time to the sound till it seemed to be moving us,
pushing us along. At one point I glanced sideways
and saw Tom's face through the bars of the cot. I
thought he was watching us but when I looked again
his eyes were closed. I closed mine. A little later Julie
decided that it was time to turn over. It was not an
easy thing to do. My leg became trapped under hers.
The bedcovers were in our way. We tried to roll one
way and almost fell off the bed and we had to roll
back. I pinned Julie's hair against the pillow with
my elbow and she said "ouch!" very loudly. We
began to giggle and forgot what we were about.
Soon we found ourselves lying side by side listening
to the great rhythmic thuds that now proceeded a
little slower than before.

Then we heard Sue calling Julie's name and
pulling at the door. When Julie let her in, Sue threw
her arms round Julie's neck and hugged her. Julie
led Sue to the bed where she sat between us,
trembling and pressing her thin lips together. I held
her hand.

"He's smashing it up," she said at last, "he found
that sledgehammer and he's smashing it up." We
listened. The thuds were not so loud now, and there
were sometimes pauses between blows. Julie got up
and locked the door and stood by it. For a while we
heard nothing. Then there were footsteps down the
front path. Julie went to the window.

"He's getting in the car." There was another long pause before we heard the engine start and the car pull away. The sharp sound of the tires on the road was like a shout. Julie pulled the curtains closed and came and sat down beside Sue and took her other hand. We sat like this, three in a row on the edge of the bed. For a long time no one spoke. Then we seemed to wake up and began to talk in whispers about Mum. We talked about her illness and what it was like when we carried her down the stairs and when Tom tried to get in bed with her. I reminded them of the day of the pillow fight when we were left in the house together. Sue and Julie had completely forgotten it. We remembered a holiday in the country before Tom was born, and we discussed what Mum would have thought of Derek. We agreed she would have sent him packing. We were not sad; we were excited and awed. We kept on breaking out of our whispers until one of us called "shhh!" We talked about the birthday party at Mum's bedside and Julie's handstand. We made her do it again. She kicked some clothes out of her way and threw herself upside down in the air. Her dark, brown limbs barely quivered, and when she was down Sue and I clapped quietly. It was the sound of two or three cars pulling up outside, the slam of doors and the hurried footsteps of several people coming up our front path that woke Tom. Through a chink in the curtain a revolving blue light made a spinning pattern on the wall. Tom sat up and stared at it, blinking. We crowded round the cot and Julie bent down and kissed him.

"There!" she said. "Wasn't that a lovely sleep?"

By the acclaimed author of
*The First Deadly Sin*
**and**
*The Second Deadly Sin*

# Lawrence Sanders

# The Sixth Commandment

The chilling story of an entire town banded together to hide a terrible truth... and of a young field investigator's efforts to unmask a doctor's reckless quest for the key to immortality itself.

**Sanders' most explosive bestseller yet!**

## Bestsellers from Berkley
## The Best in Paperback Reading

___ **THE BOOK OF MERLYN**       03826-2—$2.25
T.H. White
___ **FAT IS A FEMINIST ISSUE**    04035-6—$2.25
Susie Orbach
___ **THE FIRST DEADLY SIN**     03904-8—$2.50
Lawrence Sanders
___ **IT TAKES A LONG TIME
TO BECOME YOUNG**       04121-2—$2.25
Garson Kanin
___ **THE NEW ROGET'S THESAURUS
IN DICTIONARY FORM**     03991-9—$1.75
Ed. by Norman Lewis
___ **THE ONCE AND FUTURE KING**  04490-4—$2.95
T.H. White
___ **THE POSSIBLE DREAM**     03841-6—$2.25
Charles Paul Conn
___ **PURE AND SIMPLE**       04167-0—$2.95
Marian Burros
___ **THE SECOND DEADLY SIN**   03923-4—$2.50
Lawrence Sanders
___ **THE VISITOR**          04210-3—$2.50
Jere Cunningham

Available at your local bookstore or use this coupon for ordering:

**Berkley Book Mailing Service
P.O. Box 690
Rockville Centre, NY 11570**

Please send me the above titles. I am enclosing $_____
(Please add 50¢ per copy to cover postage and handling). Send check or
money order—no cash or C.O.D.'s. Allow three weeks for delivery.

NAME_____

ADDRESS_____

CITY_____ STATE/ZIP_____ 34